Among these unfinished tales is that of Mr. James Phillimore, who, stepping back into his own house to get his umbrella, was never more seen in this world.

—The Problem of Thor Bridge

THE DETECTIVE, THE WOMAN, AND THE WINKING TREE:
A NOVEL
OF
SHERLOCK HOLMES

Amy Thomas

Paperback ISBN 9781780923444
ePub ISBN 9781780923451
PDF ISBN 9781780923468

Published in the UK by MX Publishing
335 Princess Park Manor, Royal Drive, London, N11 3GX
www.mxpublishing.com

Cover by Mary Smiecinski

For The Baker Street Babes, my partners in crime.

Acknowledgements

The joy of writing this book was greatly enhanced by the support of my family. I am forever grateful for the unparalleled editing skills of Chris and Ashley Thomas, who gave hours of their time to help make it the best it could be. In addition, David Thomas's encouragement kept me going when I needed it most.

Designer Mary Smiecinski continues to astonish me with her artistic talent and selfless generosity. She never fails to amaze me with her ability to bring words and themes to visual life.

My two writing partners, Christy McDougall and Megan Hendrix, deserve my undying gratitude for their kindness and patience. Their friendship is a constant gift.

I am also grateful for the inspiration of my fellow Baker Street Babes, who make me laugh endlessly and think deeply about what it means to love Sherlock Holmes. I treasure their perspectives.

I also owe much appreciation to Steve Emecz of MX Publishing. His kindness, wisdom, and expertise have assisted me in many ways.

Finally, I am thankful for the many authors who have paved the way for me by writing brilliantly about Sherlock Holmes. His creator deserves the greatest praise, but behind him comes a long line of brilliant minds who have taken his creation and made him their own. This book would not have happened without their efforts.

Contents

Chapter 1…………………………….7

Chapter 2………………………...20

Chapter 3………………………...33

Chapter 4…………………...……47

Chapter 5…………………...……56

Chapter 6…………………..……68

Chapter 7………………….....……77

Chapter 8………………….....……86

Chapter 9…………………....……96

Chapter 10………………...………104

Chapter 11………………………...114

Chapter 12………………….......123

Chapter 13……………………...131

Chapter 14……………………...143

Chapter 15……………………...150

Chapter 16……………………...160

Chapter 17……………………...169

Chapter 18……………………....182

Chapter 19……………………...192

The Beginning

The wedding of Edward Cox Rayburn and Julia Ellworth Stevenson was, without a doubt, the biggest event in the village of Fulworth since Mr Percival's sheep overran the parish graveyard. I preferred the latter event—I didn't have to perform, and I was allowed to laugh. Nevertheless, I couldn't refuse when Julia's overexcited mother begged me to try to wrest something resembling music from the ancient piano in the front room of the Stevenson abode for the benefit of wedding party and guests.

I watched the crowd as I played and sang after the ceremony. Father Murphy, the vicar, stood next to the banister, eating cake and listening to Mrs Dunaway, who, from her level of animation, appeared to be extolling the virtues of her "little darling Annabel," a child of thirteen who was neither little nor darling in my estimation. The Rayburns, family of the groom, looked slightly uncomfortable in the Stevenson home. They were well aware that their son's legacy as a country farmer was not looked at with boundless favour by Charles Stevenson, a barrister who had only been moved to give his consent by several weeks of his daughter's tears. I knew this as everyone did. Villages have few secrets.

Julia herself clung to the arm of her groom and smiled radiantly, nearly as tall as her new husband. I thought her the much stronger-willed of the two, though Edward's affable grin gave a hint of the kind heart he possessed. He wasn't handsome. His face was a rough-hewn, homemade thing rather than a piece of high art, but I thought I understood his appeal.

My eyes had drifted toward the other side of the room, where, unmarried and on the prowl, Maria Ramsden was talking determinedly at the oblivious butcher, when something occurred that eclipsed even the wedding in the local consciousness. Mrs Phillimore of Oakhill Farm burst through the front door, nearly collapsing with breathlessness, her seven-year-old daughter Eliza by her side. "James is gone," she panted, as soon as she was able.

I had wondered why the Phillimores were not in attendance at the wedding. Edith Phillimore was the sort of person who never missed a chance to socialise. In contrast, her husband was taciturn and *given to moods*, as it was described locally, but seemed entirely devoted to his wife and followed her everywhere. Their absence had struck me as strange, but the events of the day had left me little time to ponder it.

The vicar was the first to react to the dramatic entrance, moving quickly toward the distraught woman and placing a large hand on her shoulder. "Gone, Mrs Phillimore? Gone where?"

"I haven't the slightest idea!" she said, looking as if she might burst into tears. "He only went inside to get his umbrella, and then—he wasn't there any more."

———

"Thanks from Colonel Digby for the return of his dog. An invitation to Lord Lewisham's party. A request to help Simon Bainbridge find out who's been stealing from him. I'll send that to Lestrade. Even he can't be fool enough to miss the secretary's obvious motive." One by one, Sherlock Holmes took up sealed envelopes, deduced their contents, and discarded them without deigning to open them.

Finally, his flatmate handed him the parcel he'd saved for last, a neat, square box covered in brown paper.

"The Woman," said Holmes quickly. "High-quality dark rosin, an early birthday gift."

"Not honey this time?" asked Watson.

"Certainly not. The shape is entirely wrong, and there's a stain on the outside of the paper where the rosin dripped." Holmes took the parcel from his friend and carefully untied the strings, revealing a box containing a tin of rosin, just as he'd expected, and, to his annoyance, a jar of honey as well. He looked up and met Watson's eye. The doctor was smiling broadly.

The detective pulled a note from the recesses of the package and, as he had not done with the rest of his post, he opened it and read the contents aloud:

Dear Mr Holmes and Dr Watson,

I hope this parcel finds you well. You will undoubtedly already have discerned that the tin of rosin is meant for Holmes, while the honey belongs to Dr Watson, who, I recall, enjoyed it immensely during your last visit.

Now for my primary purpose, which is to recount a puzzling situation. A week ago, the parish saw the wedding of a farmer's son and barrister's daughter, an occurrence overshadowed by the disappearance of a moderately prosperous farmer, who vanished without a trace as his family was preparing to leave for the ceremony. The local constabulary combed the village and surrounding country, and official reinforcements were sent from London, but none of them uncovered anything that pointed to the man's whereabouts. Knowing me as you do, you will realise that I have not been idle. I enclose a list of my observations and ask for your suggestion as to which line of enquiry I should pursue.

Yours truly,
Irene Adler

Holmes handed the second sheet of paper to his companion, who peered at it in the lamplight. "Read it to me, please," said the detective, leaning back into his chair and putting his fingertips together in front of him. Watson's steady voice filled his brain with images:

1) *The missing man, James Phillimore, is 38 years old, husband to Edith and father to Eliza.*
2) *He has been in possession of his family's farm since his father's death five years ago.*
3) *He is financially solvent but not wealthy.*
4) *Edith claims he did not seem agitated on the day of the wedding.*
5) *His disappearance occurred when he re-entered the family abode, ostensibly to fetch his umbrella, and was not seen again.*
6) *No physical evidence can be found that he left the farmhouse by the back entrance.*
7) *According to the police, the house itself shows no evidence of foul play.*
8) *No motive can be found for Edith herself to have done violence to her husband.*
9) *The umbrella is still in the house.*

"Infuriating woman," muttered Holmes, which caused his flatmate to stare with a certain amount of astonishment. "She means to lure me to Fulworth with these half-truths."

"Half-truths?"

"A great deal of surface fact, but no specifics about her observations of individuals and relationships," explained the detective. "Those she saves for my visit."

"And will you go?"

"Of course I'll go. I have nothing else on at present." Holmes glared at the frankly amused expression on his friend's face. "You will accompany me?"

"I'm afraid not." The doctor looked mildly apologetic. "I have a dinner engagement at the home of Miss Willow in three days' time." The detective did not answer, but his exit from the room was decidedly icy.

Oh, she has turned all the men's heads down in that part.

—A Scandal in Bohemia

Chapter 1: Irene

"You are a most charming woman, Miss Adler, most charming indeed," droned the nasal voice, as thick fingers wrote slowly in a yellowed notebook. "I've no doubt Inspector Graves will be delighted to hear your— observations on the case."

I had no doubt of two things. The first was that Sergeant Chipping would have been instantly less enamored of my charms if he could have heard my thoughts, and the second was that Inspector Graves, if he ever did hear my observations, would receive some version of them that would make me sound like a busybody and a fool. At such moments, I could have cursed my pretty face. Oh, how I missed Holmes, to whom facts were facts, regardless of who delivered them.

Finally, the burly policeman closed his notebook and smiled down at me, and I had the terrible premonition he intended to say something personal. I put on my iciest and most discouraging expression and was apparently successful, because he dropped his gaze and left the front room of my cottage, rather like a chastened puppy. I smiled to myself. I didn't dislike the man particularly, just his utter lack of original thought.

Ten minutes after his exit, I heard an unceremoniously loud knock at my front door. I opened it to find a tall, thin man holding a black bag and a violin case.

"Hello, Holmes," I said, failing to keep my mouth from curving up into a half-smirk.

"Good afternoon, Irene," said his low voice. "I hope you're prepared for a lodger. It's the least you can offer after your transparent effort to lure me here."

"An effort I doubted would be anywhere near so successful," I said, peering behind him. "Is Dr Watson not here?"

"Dr Watson," huffed Holmes, "is courting a Miss Willow."

"Ah," I said, thinking I understood the reason for his short temper. "Come in. Mrs Turner is shopping in the village, but I can put the kettle on."

Holmes came into the house and deposited his things in the larger of the two guest rooms, a ponderously-decorated space with dark curtains and heavy wood furnishings. It suited him quite well, I thought, and he had naturally claimed it for his own during his visits. Dr Watson always took the smaller of the guest rooms, which was lighter and more cheerful.

I made tea and took out a plate of Mrs Turner's excellent biscuits, then joined Holmes in the sitting room, where he was seated comfortably in the one gothic-looking piece of furniture I owned, a plush black wing chair.

"You look very well," he observed, with a scowl that belied his words in a comical fashion.

"As do you," I said, speaking relatively. Holmes always looked uncommonly thin, but his eyes were bright and clear, and he seemed vigorous.

"Of course I'm well," he groused, putting long fingers through his dark hair.

"Well and cross," I murmured, smiling. "But I will speak to you of the case, and perhaps that will cheer you." Holmes looked daggers at me in response to my school marm-ish tone, but I could tell that he was eager to hear the full story of the disappearance of James Phillimore. I leaned back on the flowered sofa and prepared to speak.

"Holmes, do you wish me to begin with the sequence of events, or with my assessment of what is important?" To look at my companion, it seemed as if I was speaking to a person deep in meditation or sleep, but I knew that the detective's closed eyes and relaxed body concealed a mind that was acutely aware of all it heard.

"Your discoveries, if you please," he said. "The order of events I divined from your letter and from the perusal of a local paper, which I purchased upon my arrival."

"Very well," I said, unsurprised. I knew that Holmes was not overly fond of personal conjecture, but I had rightly judged that he knew my mind's capabilities and respected its processes enough to admit space for my observations.

"As I informed you, Phillimore was last seen when his family was preparing to attend a wedding, the nuptials of Julia Stevenson and Edward Rayburn, which is where I'll begin. I had known for some time that the Stevensons did not consider Edward a suitable son-in-law, since Charles Stevenson is a barrister and had more elevated hopes for his daughter. For their part, the Rayburns were equally proud of their agricultural heritage, but they liked Julia, who did not share her family's disdain. If Charles had gotten his way, the wedding would never have taken place, but I understand from village gossip that Julia wore him down with ceaseless tears and entreaties."

I leaned forward, resting my elbows on my knees, and stared intently at Holmes, though he did not acknowledge my increased intensity in any outward way. "My acquaintance with Julia," I continued, "is not a close one, but from what I have observed of her character, I believe her desperation was played as a calculated move to

9

extract her father's blessing, rather than out of any genuine despair."

"You believe she did not love her fiancé?"

"Not so," I answered, "but I do not believe her to be the kind of woman to ever succumb to that extent of hysteria."

"Love has done stranger things to the human mind," Holmes's deep voice rejoined, "but let us move away from the uncharted territory of psychological supposition."

"Very well," I said. "I simply wished to begin by briefly sketching the characters who feature prominently in the drama."

"Continue," said Holmes, stretching out his long legs in front of him.

"The groom, Edward Rayburn, I have had occasion to meet a few times, since I often accompany Mrs Turner to purchase milk and eggs from his family's produce. He is well situated on a vast farm a few miles outside the village. I understand him to be more than able to support a wife and family. The Stevenson objection is generally known to concern his lack of elegance and social prominence, as opposed to a financial deficiency." I was silent for a moment as I bit into a chocolate biscuit and allowed the combination of sweetness and bitterness to delight my tongue.

"Almost as soon as I learned of Phillimore's disappearance, I began looking for connections between him and the families involved in the wedding, in case his absence should have to do with the particular event for which his family was bound. The associations are certainly ample, but they do not strike me as unusual. The Rayburns bought a horse from the Phillimores two months ago, and Charles Stevenson has given the Phillimore family legal advice once or twice over the past several years. Fulworth is not large, as you know, and the majority of its residents and those from the surrounding farms are connected in similar ways to one another."

"Another of my primary objectives, once it became clear that no man or corpse would be recovered easily, was to gain understanding of the missing farmer's family. Edith, his wife, is well liked in the village for her gregariousness, but her husband is known to be her opposite in temperament. I have seen him at many social events, standing near a door or side of a room, looking completely discontented until his eyes light on his wife, whom he appears to adore. Their only child, Elizabeth, is seven years old and seems uncommonly intelligent, from what I have observed."

Just then, the door opened, admitting Mrs Turner, tall and imposing in her black dress and black hat. "Good afternoon, Mr Holmes," she said, looking him up and down with a sharp eye. "You've not had anything decent to eat in weeks, I'll wager." Her disdain for Mrs Hudson's cooking was legendary, though I could not ascertain that she had ever encountered it personally. "I see you've produced tea, Miss Adler," she continued. *Produced* was the word she invariably used instead of *made* in these cases, since she believed me incapable of concocting a truly legitimate tea.

"Yes," I said, smiling. Her severity had the perverse effect of amusing me and making me adore her, a fact that I had been concerned might dismay her at the beginning of my time at the cottage. I had quickly realised, however, that for all her crossness, she enjoyed my affection.

"I hope you've brought the ingredients for one of your excellent pork pies," said Holmes, earning the ghost of a smile at the corners of the housekeeper's mouth. I laughed to myself. He knew very well that she always cooked pork pies on Monday evening. Dr Watson was particularly fond of them, and I found myself hoping that Miss Willow, whoever she might be, would accommodate him in that and other ways. I hated to think of such a kind man having any advantage taken of him.

Mrs Turner disappeared into the kitchen, a domain I was not allowed to enter when she chose to occupy it. I had tried to alter this inexorable rule a few times to offer help, but the frigid stare that greeted me had caused my resolve to evaporate. I didn't mind the arrangement. Truth be told, I had never been fond of domestic work. Some of the farm wives undoubtedly thought my retention of a housekeeper absurdly frivolous, since many households in the Fulworth area could afford little household help, even those with establishments much larger than mine.

I relaxed into the sofa cushions and heard the words "go on" issue forth from the environs of Holmes's chair, as if nothing had interrupted my story.

"I, of course, looked to the others in Phillimore's household as well. He has the managing of a moderately-sized farm that has been in his family for several generations. He inherited it upon his father's death and is assisted by a man named Peter Warren, with whom he has a complicated association."

Holmes opened his eyes briefly. "Explain."

"I have been told that until his death ten years ago, Warren's father had more or less the same position with Phillimore's father that the son currently occupies. As a result, James and Peter grew up together, attended school together in the village, and had the run of the farm. They were friends."

"David and Jonathan," murmured Holmes.

"More like Jacob and Esau," I retorted. "According to village gossip, the break in the friendship happened five years ago, when Phillimore's father died. The claim is that Warren had felt himself a part of the family for so long, especially since his own father's passing, that he had expected to be treated differently than a hired man, more as a sort of partner. Phillimore apparently did not agree and took the full birthright for himself, while offering a continued position to his friend."

"I have not spoken to Warren about his decision to stay at the farm, but the general consensus is that he couldn't bear to leave a place with so many ties and old memories. Everyone in the village knows about the disagreement, and sentiment is extremely divided. The two men rarely speak about anything other than the management of the property, though they are constantly in close proximity."

"Would Warren have anything to gain by Phillimore's death?"

"That I do not know. It seems unlikely, but I haven't yet been able to extract information about a will from anyone, since no body is in evidence."

"It's enough to begin with," said Holmes.

———

That evening, we dined on Mrs Turner's succulent pork pies, and I surmised from Holmes's healthy appetite that his mind was not yet entirely consumed by the case. Indeed not, for he talked of Paganini, and I happily joined in, enjoying the rare treat of musical discourse. After the conclusion of the meal, Holmes freed his violin from its encasing prison, caressing the smooth contours in the wood like an enchanted lover before playing a piece I had never heard before that he called *Meditation*, from a new opera by Massenet. It was exquisite.

I enjoyed watching Holmes play, as the music kidnapped the mind of the detective and made it her own. It wasn't as if he became someone else—to say so would be ridiculously limiting. No, it was as if all of the dreamy abstraction and mystery that lived behind his eyes became suddenly and starkly and beautifully evident on his face and through his fingers. Mrs Turner cried. I did not, but I understood. Once the piece was complete, Holmes played a cheerful quartet of popular beer hall dance melodies, humorously endowing them with all the gravity of a funeral dirge. Mrs Turner and I both laughed without concern for dignity, and I thought Holmes was pleased, though he did not break his comically serious character.

The housekeeper went to bed as soon as Holmes had finished, but I sat up with him and watched as his eyes drifted toward my piano in the corner. I thought perhaps he wished me to play, but I did not volunteer to do so. We sat silently for a very long time, neither of us seeking sleep or wishing to disturb the tranquil atmosphere.

"Holmes," I said after a while, "You have a performer's flair for the dramatic when you choose the juxtaposition of your violin performances. You had us crying and laughing at will."

"Yes," he said, sounding less cross than he had since his arrival, "Watson has often commented that I might have been an actor."

"There's more to it than that," I answered, looking him full in the face. "An actor parrots the lines of the playwright. When you perform, Holmes, you choose your own lines. Given your success, I'm very glad you're not a confidence man by trade."

Holmes laughed, suddenly and drily. "You are hardly less skilled in the art of manipulation. You have already succeeded in luring me here and elevating my mood. Good night, Miss Adler."

I watched the tall form leave the room and smiled to myself. Any boredom my village routine might have engendered was no longer a concern. Sherlock Holmes's presence was anything but monotonous, especially when he had a case.

Safely tucked into my own bed, underneath a quilt that had been given to me by Miss Rose from the village after I had helped her end an unfortunate liaison with a carpenter, I realised that I was more glad than sorry that Holmes had chosen to view my letter as a summons. I had not expected him, knowing that if he had an engrossing case in London, he would not be likely to put it aside for a village concern; however, I was not entirely surprised, either. No one can command Holmes when he is set against something, but he's equally resolute when he's interested in a problem. I had chosen my written words carefully, revealing enough to tantalise but also concealing much. I had attempted to manipulate him, purely and simply. He had seen through me, of course, but that had not stopped him from taking the bait. I had offered him a pretty problem, and he had thanked me by consenting to play my game, at least for the moment. I fell asleep contented.

———

The morning dawned bright, as mornings tend to do in Sussex and elsewhere. I stared at the white ceiling of my bedroom for a moment before remembering my guest in the spare room. I was glad Holmes had come, both for the sake of the investigation and for my own sake. I was happy in

Fulworth, ridiculously so, but occasionally I craved repartee with someone whose experience extended beyond the Downs, and the village afforded few such individuals. I had long since resigned myself to the fact that a certain sort of local man invariably underestimated me because of my gender, and plenty of women did as well. This could, at times, be a decided advantage if I found myself needing to extract information or achieve particular outcomes, but I preferred meeting people on an equal footing, without subterfuge if it could be avoided. Living near the coast was glorious, but sometimes I required more than invigorating scenery.

Holmes's presence was welcome, for he treated me as his experiences with me warranted. Sometimes a pretty face—not, I admit, usually a cause for complaint—could be troublesomely distracting to others. Holmes didn't even seem to see it. No, that's not quite right. He observed my face and catalogued it as part of me, the way he assimilated Dr Watson's moustache or Mrs Hudson's jet black hair. He observed, but what he observed did not prejudice him. These thoughts accompanied me as I readied myself for the day, feeling a certain air of excitement as I completed my toilette and joined Holmes at the breakfast table.

"Good morning," he said, taking a sip of coffee but not touching the vast spread Mrs Turner had provided. The long fingers of his right hand held the village's attempt at a newspaper. It was a poorly-written thing, to be sure, but certainly revelatory of local viewpoints. I often laughed at its amateurish writing style, but as a mirror reflecting popular opinion, it was without local equal.

I created what I considered stunningly beautiful artwork on my plate, consisting of liberal quantities of toast, bacon, sausage, and eggs before deigning to reply to my companion with more than a nod.

"The paper's still full of the 'Phillimore Tragedy,' as they're calling it," I observed. "It's been nearly two weeks, and without evidence of the man, people are naturally thinking of foul play."

"No one supposes him to have fled?" Holmes raised one eyebrow slightly.

"It's a hard theory to find any motive for," I admitted, "even for me. Of course, he might have been in some sort of trouble no one knew about. That seems to be the most likely cause, though I'd have thought the police might have come up with something by now if it was at all plausible. He was an enigmatic man, but one who displayed thorough devotion to his family and his duty."

Holmes nodded. "I don't share your hopeful view of the official police's capabilities, but I don't discredit your observations or conclusions. Still, such outward correctness does not always tend where it seems."

"True," I agreed. "At first, the police were enthusiastic about the idea of an escape plot, but no way was discovered for how it might have been done, and no evidence was found that he used a train or any other transportation. Edith, too, insists that he could not have fled in front of her eyes."

"And if she's lying?"

"Then she's exceptionally skilled."

"I would like to meet her," said Holmes, swirling the last dregs of coffee in the bottom of his cup as Mrs Turner glided up behind him to refill it.

"If you intend to view the scene of the disappearance, you will hardly be able to escape her," I replied, looking down and giving my full attention to my breakfast.

As he spoke the door opened and a young lady entered the room.

—The Adventure of the Copper Beeches

Chapter 2: Holmes

The detective finished his coffee in silence as his brain wove together the disparate threads of the Phillimore case into some semblance of a coherent whole. It was by no means a complete whole as of yet, but he sought something that would suggest lines of enquiry.

He was unconvinced that Phillimore was deceased. In fact, he would have been highly unsurprised to learn that the man was in London, glad to have left duty and family behind. Plenty of other men had done the same. He intended, if he was unable to ascertain the man's location himself, to enlist his brother's help. The city was a vast beehive, filled with places to hide and disappear, but Mycroft Holmes had ways of finding out people's whereabouts.

At the same time, he could not fail to acknowledge the puzzle of the case—the seemingly impossible way it had all been done. Years of dissecting crimes and criminals had taught him that crime of any sort was a nearly impossible thing to conceal in a village as small as Fulworth. Someone was sure to know something, and the police, however incompetent, invariably came up with some sort of theory. The fact that no one whatsoever had come forward and that the police had come up with nothing certainly suggested a case that had features of interest beyond the ordinary. Someone wasn't talking, someone who knew facts that were relevant to the case.

Holmes's last sip was interrupted by a nearly-imperceptible tapping on the cottage door. Neither of the two ladies heard it, for Mrs Turner was loudly washing dishes, and Irene had gone to her beehives. The detective waited a long moment and went to the door himself, a highly unusual practise, but he wanted to see the person who had chosen to announce his or her arrival in such a timid sort of way.

He opened to door to nothing—until his eyes traveled down to take in the small body of a little girl. She was of average height for a seven-year-old, with pin-straight brown hair and large grey eyes, which widened upon seeing such a large and imposing stranger. Any moment, she would bolt.

"Hello, Love, where's Mummy?" said a voice behind the child, and The Woman materialised from the direction of the hives, her chestnut hair askew and a smile on her face. She took the child's hand.

"Cottonwood's," answered the voice of the tiny person, naming a shop in the village.

"This is Mr Holmes, Eliza. He's come to visit." Irene indicated the detective with a tilt of her head.

"Hello, Mr Holmes," said the little girl seriously, taking in the stranger's dark clothing and sharp features. Holmes smiled a smile he usually reserved for the youngest members of the Baker Street Irregulars, the children he employed to prowl the London streets in search of helpful information. He was aware of his propensity to appear forbidding, a quality for which he had often been grateful, but it was one which was not universally advantageous.

"Hello, Eliza," he answered, bowing politely and extending his hand, as he would have done in the presence of royalty. He caught Irene's smile in his peripheral vision.

"You're very pointy," said the child.

"A solid observation," answered Holmes, nodding respectfully. "You have the makings of a detective."

"And you have the makings of someone far sillier than I had supposed," said Irene, grinning as she ushered the girl inside and passed her to Mrs Turner, who smiled indulgently. He followed the women inside, wondering what information he might be able to gain from the missing man's daughter.

"I've already questioned her," said Irene in a low voice at his elbow, as if she had read his mind. "She's clever, but she didn't see anything."

"Perhaps," answered the detective, "but I would still like to speak with her."

"I'm afraid you'll have to anyway. She was intrigued by you—and your angles." The Woman smirked saucily.

"I have angles enough," Holmes mused, taking his usual seat in the wing chair.

Eliza emerged from the kitchen within ten minutes, wearing traces of berry pie on her face. She stopped in the doorway when she saw Holmes and stared at him intently. The detective stared back with no less frankness. "Are you Miss Adler's friend?" asked the little girl after a long while.

"Yes," said Holmes with a wry smile. "Miss Adler and I have known each other for a long time."

"Do you live in London?"

"Yes, on a street called Baker."

"Is it very noisy?"

Holmes leaned forward slightly with his elbows on his knees and peered at Eliza from under his dark brows. "In the daytime, the air is filled with the noise of hansom cabs passing by and people selling flowers and fruit and sweets of all kinds. In the night, the darkness is broken by the sounds of horses' hooves and people yelling from too far away to understand what they say." By the time he had reached the end of this dramatically-delivered speech, he had lowered his voice to a near-whisper, and the little girl's eyes were wide open with amazement. He sat back in his chair, satisfied that he had effectively silenced her for the time being.

"Is my Papa there?" The sound of Eliza's voice disrupted the detective's complacency, and at the conclusion of her question, he looked at her with no small amount of astonishment.

"Go let Mrs Turner wash your face, and then we'll talk about it," Irene put in, and Holmes nodded to her gratefully as the little girl left the room. Once Eliza was gone, The Woman left her seat on the sofa and perched on the arm of Holmes's chair. She spoke quickly in a near-whisper. "Right after the disappearance, her mother told her that her father had gone to London and would return. Unfortunately, one of the stupider policemen assigned to the case assumed she was too young to understand and said something that made her think he was never coming back. Her mother told her it was a lie, but she's been asking about it incessantly ever since."

Holmes answered in a rapid whisper, "Normally I would advocate telling the unvarnished truth, but since the object of the obfuscation is a seven-year-old child, I can't fault the mother's reasoning. She may yet have something useful to add, though. She's certainly clever enough to have observed something significant."

"Just don't frighten her," Irene hissed into his ear before bolting back to the sofa as the child reappeared.

Holmes held out a hand to the little girl, and she came and stood in front of his chair. He took her tiny right hand in both of his and addressed her honestly. "I haven't seen your Papa, but I will work very hard to find him."

"Mr Holmes is good at finding things," said Irene.

Suddenly, the little girl became exceedingly animated. "Can you find Charles?"

"If I am to find him, you must tell me who he is," Holmes answered, as seriously as before. He stole a glance at The Woman, who simply nodded and remained silent.

"Charles," said Eliza, "is a rabbit." She looked as if anyone who was unaware of this obvious fact must be an imbecile of the highest order.

"Stuffed rabbit," Irene contributed.

Holmes allowed himself a moment to let the full absurdity of the situation pass through his consciousness, but he did not mind the humorous turn of events. The child's trust might end up proving useful, and he knew that direct interrogation was far from desirable where young children were concerned. He would allow things to unfold naturally.

Taking his small, black notebook from his pocket, Holmes began. "When did you last see Charles?"

"Last week, in Wonderland," Eliza promptly answered, exactly, Holmes thought, as if she had said "Brompton."

"How did he arrive in Wonderland?" Holmes asked, infusing all the patience he could muster into his tone. He glanced over at Irene, who appeared surprised and gratified. If The Woman thought he was unequal to managing the little girl, he would certainly prove her wrong. Small children were nothing to Scotland Yard, and sometimes, there wasn't a great deal of difference between Inspector Lestrade and a seven-year-old child.

"From the Winking Tree," said the child. "We sat down and closed our eyes and went to Wonderland, just like Papa said."

"Then what happened?" asked Holmes.

"No more Charles," said the child, with an expression of utmost dramatic woe.

Without further comment, Holmes closed his notebook and rose, taking the child's hand in his once again. "Take me to the Winking Tree."

The little girl started toward the door in an instant, pulling Holmes as if he were a dog on a leash. Irene followed, and the detective felt her amusement as if it were a living thing.

———

The Winking Tree, Holmes discovered, was in the very middle of the village, on a green in front of the local parish church. Irene did not follow him and his tiny captor all the way, instead taking a lane toward Cottonwood's to inform Edith Phillimore of her determined daughter's whereabouts. As a result, the detective found himself in the dubious position of being alone with an unfamiliar female. Age, he thought, was largely immaterial when it came to the fairer sex. A woman was a woman, as his association with Irene constantly reminded him.

As the two stepped onto the grass in front of the large beech tree, Holmes stopped the little girl with a hand on her shoulder. "Point to where you were when you went to Wonderland," he said. The child's tiny finger indicated a spot under the tree, where the grass was flattened, obviously from her seated form.

"Charles was sitting there." She pointed to a low-hanging branch.

Holmes took out his magnifying glass and scanned the ground. He knew from a conversation he had overheard on the train that the weather had been uncharacteristically dry for several days, and very little moisture had muddied the green or destroyed the imprints of shoes in the soft earth. He made out the child's prints and another set that were the size and shape of a woman's slipper. The mother's, most likely. He saw other footprints, but none of them approached the trunk of the tree. The child did not speak at all while he completed this examination, a fact that did not occur to him until he straightened back up to his full height and remembered her presence. She followed him to the base of the tree and continued to watch silently as he shifted branches and looked for any sign of the missing toy.

After a few moments of careful observation, a flash of white caught Holmes's eye. Taking a set of tiny metal forceps from his pocket, he captured the strands of white from a twisted branch. The little girl's face lit up. "That's from Charles." The inference was a logical one, but not one the detective would have expected a child to make so readily.

Holmes dropped the threads into a bag and looked for more, though he did not find any. He studied the tree and the ground for a few moments more before taking Eliza's hand and turning back the way they had come. They found Irene at the edge of the green, joined by a short, plain woman in grey. Eliza broke free of the detective's grasp and ran to her mother, whose smile transformed her face into something nearly pretty.

A quick study of Edith Phillimore revealed to Holmes that she was genuinely worried about her missing husband, a fact he had desired to ascertain for certain before he made further judgements. Her eyes were rimmed with darkness in her pale face, and her dress showed signs of a lack of care that belied the good quality of the fabric, a lack of care she had not displayed when clothing her child. Even as she embraced Eliza, her gaze scanned the village, as if she thought she might yet see some clue she had missed. After a moment's observation, the detective was willing to concede that Edith's concern over James was natural and unaffected. He caught Irene's eye, and her small look of triumph seemed to indicate that she understood his thoughts.

The Woman introduced her friends to one another, and Edith smiled tensely. "Mr Holmes, thank you for your kindness to my daughter."

"It was no trouble," answered the detective. He leaned down to the little girl. "Miss Eliza, I'm sorry I cannot produce Charles immediately, but I hope to be able to do so very soon." Eliza nodded and stared at him with her large eyes.

"May we come to your house?" Irene asked, ending the awkward silence that followed. "Mr Holmes would like to see it."

Edith nodded. "I doubt that you will find anything the police missed." Her voice was terse, almost bitter.

"Perhaps," said Holmes, "but I have been known to do so in the past." He thought he heard the slightest hint of a snort come from The Woman, but he said nothing else as he followed the women and child away from the green.

———

Holmes's first glimpse of Oakhill Farmhouse was unsurprising. The house was a square, two-storey structure with a chimney and two rows of front windows. It was clearly the home of a moderately prosperous family, neither mean nor opulent.

He alighted from the Phillimores' wagon and offered his assistance to Eliza, who giggled as he swung her to the ground. In the meantime, Irene and Edith alighted with the help of a large, grey-bearded man and joined the detective and the little girl in front of the house while the man led the horse away toward the nearby barn.

"That's Styles," said Edith. "He's been here forever."

"Mrs Phillimore," the detective began, "would you mind taking me through the particulars of the day your husband disappeared?"

"Yes, of course," she answered. "Eliza, show Miss Adler how big the chickens are getting." Irene understood this to be her cue and submitted to being dragged away by the little girl, a fate Holmes knew she relished, judging by the sanguine expression on her beautiful face.

"It's probably silly of me, Mr Holmes," Edith continued, "but I don't like to speak of it before her. Not until—not until we know something for certain." Holmes didn't answer, but he considered how typical it was of parents to underestimate the understanding of children. He would have bet money on the fact that Eliza knew far more than her mother realised.

"Miss Adler has probably told you that the whole village was invited to the Stevenson wedding. I dressed Eliza in the morning while my husband did chores with the men, and he finally readied himself with only moments to spare. Styles brought the carriage around for us, but James said it looked like it might rain and that we'd better have an umbrella with us, so he went back inside. That was all, and then he wasn't there."

"Was there no one in the house at the time that your husband returned to it?"

"No, I had given the maid the day off. She was a friend of the bridal household and wanted to help with preparations. The cook left for the wedding just before we did."

"Where exactly was the carriage brought?"

"The same place where we left the wagon just now."

"How long was it before you became alarmed?"

"Well, my husband keeps his umbrella in a large carved vase by the door, so I expected him to emerge within a few seconds. When he didn't, I thought it was strange, but I waited until nearly ten minutes had elapsed. At that point, I was more irritated than worried. I couldn't imagine what was keeping him. I told Eliza to stay in the carriage, and I walked back into the house, but James wasn't there."

"I'd like you to retrace your steps, please, as nearly as you can remember them."

"I remember them well," she said. "I've had to repeat them to the police many times."

"I am reasonably convinced that this time will produce better results."

She half smiled, but her voice was brittle. "It was very kind of you to come here, Mr Holmes. I'm sure you have far more important things to do than look for one missing farmer."

"Not in the least," answered the detective. "I came because the case interested me, and I will not leave it unsolved." Edith looked unconvinced as she led him into the house.

The first thing that caught Holmes's eye was a large wooden receptacle with two umbrellas sticking out of it. "His umbrella was never touched," said Edith.

"Interesting," said Holmes. He did not utter them aloud, but his brain immediately catalogued the available options: either Phillimore had never intended to fetch the umbrella at all, or whatever had happened to him had occurred before he had a chance to pick it up. The third option, that Phillimore or someone else had picked it up and then replaced it, he considered possible but unlikely.

Edith led him through to a parlour with a piano, a sofa, and a few hard-looking chairs. There were no signs of a struggle, but Holmes wished devoutly that he had been on hand more quickly, before the police had obliterated most of the potential evidence. Still, even the regular force was usually competent enough to see the signs of a fight, and the woman of the house seemed too intelligent to have missed them herself.

"May I see the upstairs, please?" he asked, after an extensive perusal of the room. "You may leave me to my own devices." Holmes uttered the phrase in a tone that left no doubt of his desire to be left alone to complete his observations. Edith nodded once and left the room. The two weeks since her husband's disappearance had apparently acclimated her to the invasion of her home by unfamiliar and unwanted guests, though the set of her shoulders indicated that she still felt slight displeasure at the intrusion.

Holmes made his way up the modest staircase, noting the presence of obligatory portraits of stern-looking relatives, and found himself in a long hallway with rooms on either side. He began at one end, entering a room that obviously belonged to a servant. Its furnishings were neat but meagre, and no personal objects were in sight other than a small, cheap mirror with a cracked silver handle. He quickly searched the small, rough-hewn wardrobe before leaving the room and proceeding down the hall.

Two other similar rooms completed the accommodations of the live-in staff, and Holmes determined that, depending on the conclusions of his findings in the house, he might also contrive ways to enter the homes of the farm hands and their wives to see if their occupants might be inclined to tell tales of what they knew.

The detective set his steps toward the family rooms, ready to uncover any detail the police had missed. Nearly two weeks was a long time—for a wife to hide whatever she did not wish to be seen, for the careless tread of policemen to obscure delicate clues, or for a resourceful criminal to destroy evidence. But Holmes knew himself, and he was equal to the task.

Detection is, or ought to be, an exact science and should be treated in the same cold and unemotional manner.

—The Sign of Four

Chapter 3: Irene

The chickens looked exactly as they had every time I had submitted to having them shown to me. More than anything, my acquaintance with Eliza Phillimore had reminded me of the astonishing, stubborn love of repetition that exists in childhood, until adulthood robs us of the wonder of sameness.

I knelt down obediently beside the little girl and watched as the largest chicken, which was named Mrs Merriwether after the family's rotund cook, pecked mercilessly at the tiny rooster, who was known as Rogers. I watched the child, too, wondering how much she knew or could possibly suspect about her father's disappearance. Her mother never spoke of it to her, but I wondered if that was the best course of action, given that he might never return.

Presently, Eliza's seven-year-old mind tired of chickens, and she dragged me toward the large, weather-beaten barn, which was as grey as her eyes. "Miss Adler," she said, pulling my hand as if it were a toy, "is Mr Holmes nice?"

A host of amusing thoughts crowded into my mind, but I answered honestly, "Mr Holmes is interesting, and that's even better." I bent down to adjust my shoe and hide the laugh that I couldn't keep from coming. Eliza stopped, too, and fingered a blade of green grass as if it were the most exquisite lace.

I had only been inside the barn once, a year before, when Eliza had insisted on showing me a newly-born foal, but it had not changed since I had seen it. The same smell of manure assaulted my nose, and the same men, busily at work, stopped just long enough to nod in my direction. I felt the crunch of hay under my feet and heard the sounds of horses in the yard beyond. My eyes were fascinated by a building that was immense, but at the same time filled with all manner of nooks and crannies and tiny spaces. I wondered how many of them had been the recipients of Eliza's tiny body and what she might have seen and heard while resident in them.

I noticed with interest that Peter Warren, known locally for his bitter conflict with Phillimore, was in one corner of the barn—off to himself, polishing a leather instrument that I did not recognise. Holmes would want to speak to him; of that I was sure. For myself, I couldn't help thinking that the man's severe, spare appearance did not indicate a charitable temperament, though that did not necessarily indicate murderous intent.

Eliza didn't utter a word until she had brought me through the barn and into the smaller carriage house, which was connected by a side door and opened onto the yard. It was dark and quiet, and once we had passed into it, we found ourselves alone. "This is Eliza's place," said my companion, pointing to a tiny, claustrophobic corner behind the family's one ancient carriage. It held a small, tattered blanket spread out over straw, a tin of biscuits, a yellowed lace shawl, and a picture book. Eliza sat down, and I crouched beside her, wondering why she had chosen to let me into her tiny world. She arranged a straw throne for me, and I stretched out my legs and leaned against the structure's ancient back wall, wondering what discoveries Holmes might be making inside the house.

"Charles!"

In the dark, serene atmosphere of the carriage house, the child's shocked screech nearly made me let out an answering scream, but I recovered myself and looked over to find her clutching a grimy, stuffed white rabbit to her chest.

"Where did you find him?" I asked, slightly perplexed. I knew Holmes would have found it unforgiveable, but I had allowed myself to drift off and miss the moment of discovery.

"He was under here," she said, lifting up the edge of her tiny blanket.

"Ah, you must have forgotten and left him here," I said, in the exact knowing way that had irritated me when adults had used it during my own childhood.

"No!" she said, shaking her head vehemently. "I looked." I stared at her a moment, trying to evaluate the truth of what she was saying. If she were right, then things had certainly taken a peculiar turn. I resolved to let Holmes decide.

"Let's go back to the house and show Mummy," I said brightly, hoping to lure the child without a fight. In her usual fashion, she took my hand wordlessly and began to pull me back toward the house, clasping the rabbit in her other hand. I considered that if the toy were actual evidence, then Holmes would probably fault the fact that I had not seized it, but I didn't relish trying to pry the prodigal rabbit from Eliza's eager clutches.

The quick trot to the house gave me enough time to consider the implications of a disappearing stuffed rabbit. I tried to think like Holmes. How small did a coincidence have to be before it was allowable? Was a child's mysteriously-appearing toy insignificant enough to be unrelated to the disappearance of her father? I did not have Holmes's knack for weaving together the seemingly unrelated strains of a problem. I could understand events as they occurred, but I could not always perceive their interconnectedness.

Eliza and I found her mother in the farmhouse kitchen, joining the cook in the preparation of lunch. She looked up in surprise as we entered, though her face was not unpleasant. I would not have inserted myself unceremoniously into the kitchen of every home in Fulworth, but the Phillimores had never kept a formal household.

"Mummy, I've found Charles!" burst immediately from Eliza's throat, sparing me from having to explain the situation. In excited tones, she explained the circumstances of the rabbit's sudden reappearance, all the while cuddling it in irrepressible joy. I watched Edith carefully, thinking Holmes would want me to catalogue her reaction as closely as I could.

She seemed genuinely surprised, and after a moment, she looked up and met my gaze solidly. "I can attest that she looked there before. We searched it together right after she lost him." I nodded, wondering what Holmes would make of it.

I didn't have long to ponder the question, because the detective soon appeared with a wide-eyed young housemaid in tow. "The tone of voices I heard across the house indicates that something of import has occurred," he said mildly, smiling benignly but in a way that suggested to me his annoyance at having missed something.

"Charles has reappeared," I intoned softly. Holmes's eyes flashed triumph for a split second before he resumed his air of harmless pleasantry.

"May I see Charles, please?" he asked, bending down to Eliza's level. I thought the child might be reluctant to give up her recently-regained treasure, but her nascent fondness for my angular friend won out, and she handed the rabbit to him readily. Her mother was just behind her, and I almost thought I saw her flinch, but the impression made no sense to me at the time, so I pushed it aside.

————

Holmes and I returned to my cottage in silence. I knew him well enough to tell that he was deep in thought, and I had no desire to awaken his irritation by disturbing him, though I dearly desired to know what he had made of the recent events.

As we approached the front door, he seemed to remember my existence and looked down at me with a smile—his genuine one, not the falsely benign one of the morning. "I didn't think things would move so quickly," he mused contentedly, as if he were commenting on the weather. I resisted the urge to pinch him.

"What things do you mean?"

"I didn't suppose the rabbit would be returned so quickly," he said. "Certainly not when we were present. Mrs Phillimore nearly turned green when I touched the thing. I assume you observed her reaction."

"I did," I said coolly, trying not to sound as if I had almost discarded the observation as irrelevant. "I didn't understand it, though," I added unashamedly.

"No," said Holmes, "and I believe she thought me equally befuddled, but I was far from it."

"Of course," I rejoined archly. "The great Sherlock Holmes is never befuddled by anything."

"Very few things," he answered in dead earnest, though I caught a faint twinkle in his bright eyes.

"I see that you're brimful of curiosity," he continued. "I'm no less curious about your experiences with the child, but I assume you'll require some sort of edible nourishment before you'll be able to manage complicated conversation."

"Indeed," I answered, laughing to myself. I wanted to think of some withering reply, but in truth, I was starving, and my brain didn't wish to cooperate. Thankfully, as we entered the house, it was immediately apparent that Mrs Turner had seen us coming up the hill, for she was setting out a meal of boiled eggs and cold meat.

Holmes did not join me at the table, electing instead to make his way to his chair in the sitting room. Mrs Turner's annoyance at this amused me, since she was certainly well acquainted with my companion's tendencies, but I said nothing. I was too busy eating eggs and regaining a sense of mastery over the world.

Once I'd had my fill of luncheon, I joined Holmes, who was reading over pages in his small notebook. "You look better," he said without looking up.

"You look attentive," I answered.

"And therein lies one of the chief differences between you and Watson," Holmes intoned, his gaze still on the page before him. "When he points out the obvious, he simply means to draw attention to it. When you point it out, you mean something else entirely."

"Exactly," I answered, "and what I mean to say now is that I'm going to burst if you continue to be cryptic and uncommunicative."

"Very well," said the detective, shutting his book and sitting back in the wing chair like a king on his throne, with his fingertips pressed together in their usual position. "I expect you observed that the ground floor of the home bears no evidence of a physical struggle. I can add that the upstairs is similarly without such signs. Of course, Edith

Phillimore would have had ample time to try to obscure them if she'd wished, but doing so with absolute completeness is nearly impossible for accomplished criminals, let alone amateurs." (I sniggered at the way he said "amateurs," as if crime were analogous to sport.)

"No," he continued, "I became convinced fairly quickly that Phillimore's disappearance had been, if not willing, at least effected through means that did not incite a struggle."

"A chemical anesthetic would have had to be administered and then Phillimore's inert body would have had to be dragged out of the house, I suppose," I said, thinking aloud.

"Just so," said Holmes, "and there was no evidence of that either, on top of the fact that the process would have required the kidnapper coming up to the farmhouse, which would have alerted Mrs Phillimore and anyone else who was around the property at the time."

"It looks bad for Edith, then," I mumbled.

"Yes," said Holmes, "though consideration of her potential involvement presents its own set of problems. If she killed Phillimore in the house, for instance, then she certainly did it in the least messy and most efficient way possible and without leaving any evidence whatsoever, a practically impossible feat, on top of which is the question of what she did with the body."

"Could she have lured him outside and done it?"

"Possibly, but the property was far from deserted when she departed for the wedding. I intend to question the man Styles to corroborate her timeline of events, but if she was honest about how quickly everything took place, then the realm of possibility narrows."

"He will corroborate it," I said, glad that I had something to add. "One of the reasons Edith wasn't badgered even more by the police was because of his statement. He said that he brought the carriage, saw husband and then wife re-enter the house, and then finally saw Edith drive away very quickly. He wondered where Phillimore was, but said he didn't think too much of it because Edith often drove herself and the child, and everyone in the village knows that James Phillimore has his moods."

"It's an attractive problem," said Holmes, sounding far from displeased. "Usually, people disappear from public places or open spaces. A house leaves such little room for error, either on the part of the perpetrator of the disappearance or the investigator."

"Aren't you going to ask how I learned the man's story?" I asked.

"Not at all," said Holmes. "I already know. The two possibilities are that you asked him yourself, or you found out from the police. If the former, you couldn't be sure that he had told you exactly what he told them. The latter, then. You asked Sergeant Chipping, and he, being enchanted by your face in the usual way, told you everything you wanted to know."

"How did you deduce that?" I asked, slightly impressed, though not overmuch shocked, knowing Holmes as I did.

"The day I arrived, I saw a sheet of paper in the bin in your cottage. It was the size and shape of the usual contents of a police notebook. It had your name at the top and the beginning of a line of text, and then the writer's pen obviously ran out, at which time he scratched over the paper to try to force ink to flow but was unsuccessful, leading to the discarding of the page. From that I deduced that a policeman had been in your house and taken some kind of statement from you. I could hardly believe you had given information without taking plenty in return, even if the man was unaware of it."

"And Chipping? How did you know it was him?"

"The newspaper mentioned an Inspector Graves and a Sergeant Chipping as being connected to the investigation. The inspector would be unlikely to take time to conduct the interview himself, no matter how much your observations might have actually warranted his attention. He would have considered it beneath his notice and sent one of his subordinates instead. It was simply a matter of probability."

I was reminded of the many times that Dr Watson, after hearing his flatmate's chain of reasoning, had declared it to be simple after all. It was, and yet it wasn't. Anyone could see the links; few could chain them together into something that held up. Holmes could.

"True," I said simply. "But what about the stuffed rabbit?"

"What about the stuffed rabbit?" Holmes echoed. "My perusal of the tree revealed that Eliza and her mother were the only ones who had approached the place where the child fell asleep. In that case, the rabbit had to have been removed by Eliza, her mother, or by someone else, but using a tool that would allow him or her to grasp it without approaching the tree. Such an action would have been pointless; unless the person expected an immediate and detailed investigation, there would be no reason to avoid approaching the tree. The fibres I found in the branches indicated, too, that someone had carefully grasped the rabbit rather than wrenching it with an apparatus, which would almost certainly have left far more residue. I concluded, then, that Edith had removed Charles while her daughter slept."

I stared at my friend. "Why in the world would she have done such a thing?"

"In time, Miss Adler," said Holmes, unable to suppress a slight smile. "I will elaborate in an orderly fashion." The detective leaned back slowly, and I secretly wished I could simply read Dr Watson's version of the tale and skip to the significant parts—Holmes, of course, found all details significant in some way.

I pursed my lips as Holmes continued. "My conclusions about the probability of the rabbit's disappearance indicated to me that Mrs Phillimore knew more than she had revealed to anyone. She showed the appropriate signs of genuine worry for her missing spouse, but from then on, my communications with her were tests of sorts. You asked if we might visit the house, and she consented. From that, I inferred that she expected either to be able to keep me from discovering evidence in her home or else that she believed there was none to be found. I also noted that despite the local description of her as exceptionally gregarious, she did not appear so at all when she spoke to me. Could a missing husband account for this discrepancy? Perhaps, but it has been my experience of many years that even the most extreme calamity doesn't change a person's demeanor completely, especially after several days have passed."

"Most people give many allowances of temper to one who is perceived to be in distress or grief, as you and the villagers have done with Edith Phillimore, but her manner was too studiedly depressed for one of normally sanguine disposition, even in a time of difficulty. In other words, I began to believe that a portion of her behaviour was affected. And yet—" Holmes's eyes gleamed, and I could see that he was enjoying himself—"she didn't seem completely disingenuous. Her look and movement betrayed real concern, though she took care to emphasise it purposefully."

"You were not present for my next test of our hostess, which was to request to examine the upstairs of the home on my own. If she had been concerned with a need to direct my investigations, she would have balked at this, but she was willing, if somewhat short of congenial. Nevertheless, I conducted my examinations in the usual way. Just because someone believes that no evidence is present does not mean that it is actually the case. The police's inability to turn anything up was equally insignificant in my mind, given the official force's common inability to discover anything that is out of plain sight."

"Did you find anything?" I asked, trying to trick the least susceptible man in the world into hurrying his narrative.

"I began in the servants' rooms," said Holmes, exactly as if I hadn't spoken. "I saw nothing out of the ordinary. The family rooms, too, seemed to corroborate the wife's claim that her husband had taken nothing with him, though it was a difficult assertion to either prove or disprove without an intimate knowledge of the man's possessions. It was not until I was nearing the conclusion of my investigation of the man's own room that I found one significant absence: tobacco."

"How did you know he used it regularly?" I asked, finding it unnecessary at that moment to affirm that I had seen the missing man smoking a pipe on more than one occasion.

"Telltale signs," he said. "Dusting of the stuff around the room, the lingering odor. Most significantly, the surface of the side table beside Phillimore's bed revealed a trace of ash next to the faint outline of a commonly-sized tobacco pouch, as if it had been laid there regularly for several years. If nothing whatsoever had been moved in the room, then where was the pouch? Edith's claim to police and local newspaper was, as you know, unequivocal—Her husband, she said, carried nothing with him when he returned to the house except the clothes he wore."

I was so interested in Holmes's tale that the insistent knock at my cottage door seemed unreal at first. I didn't move until it sounded a second time, the rapping of a fist that obviously had no lack of physical force behind it. I was already at the door when Mrs Turner emerged from the kitchen, and I opened it to find a blue-eyed officer of the law.

"Good afternoon, Sergeant Chipping," I said automatically, my brain whirring through any possible reasons he might have for coming back to my house in spite of the force's obvious disdain for my feminine observations. I hoped fervently that his mind was not amorously inclined, as I had previously feared.

"Good afternoon, Miss Adler," he said, his gaze moving past me to take in Holmes, who had joined me in his noiselessly graceful way.

"This is my friend, Mr Sherlock Holmes," I said by way of an awkward introduction.

"The detective?" Chipping seemed bewildered for a moment, but he shook his large head and went on. "I've come about Mrs Phillimore. They've found her husband's body, and she asked us to notify you, Miss Adler. She's very shaken up, you may imagine."

44

"What?" I uttered.

A minute examination of the circumstances served only to make the case more complex.

—The Adventure of the Empty House

Chapter 4: Holmes

The Woman was obviously shocked. Holmes stepped forward and smiled at the young policeman. "Where is the body?" he asked evenly.

"They found him at his farm," he answered, "in the carriage house."

"Didn't the police look there before?"

"Yes, Sir," said Chipping. "I looked through the place myself. He wasn't there a week ago, right after he went missing." Holmes was glad the young man wasn't tight-lipped.

"Quite right, I'm sure," he answered. "Miss Adler will follow you to Mrs Phillimore."

"Inspector Graves sent a wagon for her," said Chipping, looking over at Irene's white face quizzically, "if she cares to come along."

"As long as Mr Holmes accompanies us," said The Woman suddenly. Holmes almost laughed aloud. She might be momentarily stunned, but Irene Adler never really lost her wits.

"Of course, if you wish," said Chipping uncertainly, obviously weighing his options and finding the prospect of refusing a distraught lady beyond his sensibilities.

"Thank you," murmured Irene faintly, and Holmes could tell that she was making the most of her influence over the sergeant.

The detective held Irene's arm as they followed Chipping outside, trying to assist her in continuing her appearance of frail femininity in case either of them should need its advantage as the afternoon progressed. If the policeman wondered what a famed London detective was doing in Irene Adler's house, he didn't betray his curiosity, instead retaining his businesslike manner as the three situated themselves for the short journey to the farm.

———

As Holmes surveyed the Phillimore farmhouse for the second time in one day, he took in an atmosphere that was radically different from the one of the morning. There were people everywhere—workmen, police, and women from the village loitering around the edges, trying to grasp whatever morsels of information they could. It was always the same in villages. Nothing could be concealed, and nearly everyone could be on hand in moments, it seemed. The detective took in every face and the manner of every observer, storing them in his memory in case he should need to recollect them.

Holmes followed Sergeant Chipping through the gawking crowd, noting recognition in the eyes of a few who had seen him on previous visits to Fulworth, though he had never made an effort to enter village life. Irene was more communicative, speaking subdued greetings to those she knew, as befit the circumstances.

Only a small group had been allowed inside the house, and the body had been laid out in the front parlour, Around it stood an elderly man who was obviously a doctor, a policeman Holmes knew to be Inspector Graves, a well-dressed gentleman he did not recognise, a hired man, and the widow, who looked as shocked as anyone Holmes had ever seen. His first task as he stepped into the room was to scrutinise her face, but he could no longer detect any sign that she was exaggerating her feelings. Whatever she might or might not know about her husband's disappearance, his death had caught her off guard.

"Holmes?" The police inspector looked up and met the detective's eyes, his face a mask of irritated surprise.

"Good afternoon, Inspector," said Holmes evenly, concealing his repugnance.

"Sergeant Chipping," said Graves, ignoring the detective, "I told you to bring Miss Adler," *and no one else* was implied by his chilly tone of voice.

The unfortunate younger policeman cleared his throat and answered deferentially. "The lady took a turn when she heard the news, Sir. She asked for her friend to come along."

Inspector Graves looked as if he might devour his subordinate on the spot. "Very well," he sputtered. "Mr Holmes can help Miss Adler keep Mrs Phillimore company."

Edith Phillimore looked up as if she had just noticed their entrance and walked over to Irene in a daze. The Woman took her hand. "Let's go to the kitchen," she said gently.

"You'll have to go, too, Mr Holmes," said Graves in his high-pitched voice. "Only those with official business can stay."

"Very well," said Holmes, in no mood to argue. At the present time, he had more interest in seeing the place where the dead man had been found than in seeing the corpse itself. Graves's preoccupation with the body meant the detective's chances of examining the carriage house were far higher than if the inspector had been roaming the grounds himself.

Holmes followed Irene, who led Edith to a chair in the kitchen. He smiled at the family's lone housemaid, whose acquaintance he had made earlier in the day. She seemed to be hiding in the recesses of the small room, trying to fade into the corner. The cook was not in evidence.

Edith stared at her hands for a few seconds before speaking. "Peter Warren found him," she said softly. "He had gone to fetch one of the wagons, and there James was, seated on top of the carriage with a blanket around him and a bullet through his forehead." She laughed a short, stabbing laugh, and then she cried. Irene knelt down and put an arm around her. Holmes slipped out quietly, making his way from the house.

When the detective arrived at the carriage house, he found Chipping inside, supervising two policemen who looked young enough to be schoolboys. He nodded to the three officers of the law, but the sergeant looked uncertain. "No one's supposed to be in here," he began, clearing his throat.

"I won't disrupt your work," said Holmes, cutting him off genially and thinking to himself that the work being performed, which included much stamping about and stroking of surfaces, had more to do with destroying evidence than collecting it. Chipping relaxed a little, and a smile crossed his thickly amiable face.

"I suppose it won't hurt anything."

"Very wise," Holmes intoned, careful to stand out of the way of the concentrating boy policemen, who had ceased moving and were staring hard at the ground as if it might open its mouth and utter something profound. "Is that where he was found?" The detective's eyes traveled to the top of a large hulk of a carriage, the sort that had, by its obvious age, been passed down through the family over several years.

"Right there!" came the overly enthusiastic voice of one of the investigating infants, a short lad with sandy hair, who dropped his gaze as soon as he had spoken, as if he was abashed by the sound of his own voice.

Chipping nodded gravely. "Sitting up there like he was going to drive away any second. Gave the man who found him quite a turn."

"Who found him?" Holmes asked, enquiring about a fact he already knew as a further test of the sergeant's good humour.

"Hired help by the name of Peter Warren," came the reply. After a moment, the policeman dropped his voice and added, "No love lost between him and the dead man, they say." Holmes realised that the large young man had begun to consider him an ally.

The detective's mind started to tease out strands of the web. A murderer might try to avert suspicion by finding the corpse himself, but Warren's part in the drama certainly changed the look of things.

After a short time, Chipping and his subordinates left, consenting to give Holmes a few minutes alone. The detective shook his head in exasperation at the police footprints that covered the floor and the evidence of interference on nearly every surface. Still, he was determined to discover what he could.

Systematically, he walked a perimeter around the carriage, then climbed onto it. The one place the policemen hadn't touched was where the corpse itself had rested, and he saw where the dust had been displaced. With irritation, he realised that he couldn't ascertain how the body had been placed there because it was impossible to distinguish evidence of the murderer's movements from the police's. From atop the carriage, though, he was able to visualise the possible entrances and how the corpse might have been conveyed.

After a few moments, Holmes jumped down and walked outside by way of the entrance that faced the house. He saw with relief that the police had managed to get rid of the village crowd and that no one else was in sight. He scanned the area, and, when he was satisfied, returned to the farmhouse and entered it by the staff entrance.

Just inside, he found a man waiting for him. "Peter Warren," barked the newcomer gruffly, inclining his head toward a small room near the kitchen, a dirty place where the household staff kept their shoes and coats. Holmes followed him inside, bracing himself for anything; an attempted punch wouldn't have surprised him, nor would a flood of tears. What he did not expect was for the man's face to break into a friendly smile. "I'm glad it's you, Mr Holmes," was next, followed by a proffered hand. It took the detective a moment to accept the enthusiastic handshake, though years of practise allowed him to disguise his surprise.

"I'm equally pleased, Mr Warren," he said smoothly, "given your unique vantage point on the day's events." The man smiled again, an action that seemed somewhat foreign to his face, and motioned to Holmes to sit down on a rickety wooden bench, while he occupied a chair opposite.

"The thing is, Mr Holmes, I don't know how they done it," he began.

"In that, you are not materially different from the majority of the rest of the world," said Holmes drily, beginning to feel irritated.

"It's just, how did it get there without no one seeing it?" said the hired man.

"Perhaps you might begin at the beginning," said Holmes, carefully keeping his tone level.

"I was on the other side of the barn from the carriage house—it was just me and Simmons—and I told him to go off for something to eat. He went back to the house; the men who live further away eat there. My Em and I live closer, so I usually go home. I decided to walk through the carriage house, and there he was. I didn't know he was dead at first."

"What did you do then?"

"I called to him and then climbed up and saw the bullet in his forehead. I think—I might have figured it out sooner if I hadn't been shaken up. I didn't know what I was seeing at first."

"Continue," Holmes murmured, finally engrossed in the man's tale.

"That's about all. I went back to the house and raised the alarm—"

"To whom, exactly?" put in the detective's deep voice.

"I saw the cook, Mrs Merriwether, and she told the rest of the house."

"I see," said Holmes, opening his eyes for the first time in several moments to find the hired man nodding intently.

"That were—exactly like you do it in the stories, Mr Holmes, as if you're asleep, but I'll wager you heard every word." Not for the first time in his existence, a certain number of uncharitable thoughts toward his loquacious flatmate entered Holmes's mind, but he dismissed them as irrelevant to the present problem and returned his focus to the matter at hand.

"You must know, Mr Warren, that you are a prime suspect," he said sharply, watching the man's face to ascertain his response.

Warren went slightly pale, but he answered after a moment. "That'd be a strange way for a murderer to act, wouldn't it, finding the corpse for the police?"

"Killers have done odder things," Holmes rejoined, "but you're not a murderer. Still, it's going to take some doing to make the police as firmly convinced of that as I am. They're unlikely to take my word for it." He met Warren's eyes for a moment.

"You played your cards well by speaking to me. Keep playing them well, and you may avoid the noose." The detective left the room.

No; he is not a man that it is easy to draw out, though he can be communicative enough when the fancy seizes him.

—A Study in Scarlet

Chapter 5: Irene

I am not the sort of person who goes around comforting people in their every distress. Fulworth, like all other villages in the world, I'll wager, has its share of people who leap at the chance to feed off tragedy, but I find that a quiet word or a smile a few weeks after something has occurred is usually more welcome. I am not, however, without feeling.

As I held Edith Phillimore, I understood the spectacular aloneness that can sometimes crowd around a popular person. Edith was known everywhere in town and by everyone, but she was close to no one. She had called for me because I was the closest thing she had to a friend, the other woman in town whom everyone knew but no one knew well. The difference was that I had chosen my aloneness intentionally, while she seemed to fight against hers with every fake laugh she uttered.

After a few minutes, I thought of Eliza, and I felt a pang of guilt that she hadn't crossed my mind sooner. I looked up over Edith's bowed head and mouthed a question to the maid, who mouthed back *outside with cook*. I wondered where the woman was keeping her, and the question bothered me enough that I started to contrive a way to settle the mother so that I could find the daughter.

Edith obeyed me with the compliance of a dazed child when I shepherded her upstairs, and the timid maid helped me get her into bed. I left the girl, who did not seem unintelligent, with instructions to stay by Edith's bedside until the doctor appeared.

I made my way downstairs with a determined step, knowing that I was about to re-enter a decidedly male domain. I saw no reason to create conflict without purpose, but I never had any trouble asserting myself when the situation demanded, or should I say suggested it, as Holmes was well aware from our previous encounters.

Indeed, as I stepped into the parlour, I could practically feel the ice in the stares that greeted me. Having been banished to my proper female sphere, I was neither expected nor welcome to return to this one. Thankfully, I have been plenty of places in my life where I was not welcome, and the impression has had no lasting effect on me except a lingering sense of amusement. I smiled at the police inspector and then addressed Dr Clarke, who was still studying the body. "I've put Mrs Phillimore to bed. I believe she might benefit from a sleep aid of some kind." He stared at me for a moment, and then nodded wordlessly and left the room, clearly irritated at my interference, but even more so by the fact that my suggestion was undeniably reasonable.

"Very good, Miss Adler," came a voice from the recesses of the room, and I looked over to find Julia Stevenson's father coming toward me, using every inch of his considerable height to intimidate me as much as possible. Charles Stevenson always seemed to be looking down at one from a physical and moral height of some sort, as if he saw a flaw in every character but his own—and his daughter's, for he doted on her. I realised he had been in the room when Holmes and I had first entered the house. An unpleasant man, but I supposed he might be useful under the circumstances, since he had a great deal of legal knowledge.

I excused myself quickly, much to the relief of Inspector Graves, who looked as though he would have liked to arrest me for something but couldn't think of any legitimate reason. I determined to ask Holmes about the man's obvious dislike of him at the earliest possible opportunity. Graves wasn't the most delightful of men at any time, but seeing Holmes had brought something out in him that I had not previously observed.

Holmes's whereabouts didn't concern me. Knowing him as I did, I expected that he would be at the scene of the discovery, taking in the details that would have eluded me. My mind, instead, turned to concern for Eliza. The maid had offered no suggestions, but I had an idea of my own: the chicken house.

Sure enough, I wasn't forced to employ my skills of deduction any further. The portly cook and the little girl were right where I had expected, in the midst of the hens, Eliza looking as if nothing in the world had ever been so enjoyable, and the cook looking as if she'd like very much to be elsewhere.

The bright face the child turned toward me suggested that she knew nothing of what had transpired, and I didn't know whether to be glad or sorry. Mrs Merriwether was certainly a poor choice to be the bearer of terrible news, but the truth couldn't wait forever.

"Eliza," I said suddenly, "how would you like to stay at my house on the hill tonight?" Her face turned serious, and she nodded in wonder, as if the idea was beyond her comprehension. I smiled as brightly as I could and took her hand. "Come inside, and we'll get your things ready."

The cook was obviously relieved. She seemed to have expected Eliza to be her personal charge for the foreseeable future, and my willingness to take on that dread duty earned the one and only smile I ever received from her during our acquaintance.

I, of course, did not normally find Eliza an onerous duty. Her inquisitive mind and willingness to explore any subject made her, I thought, a far better companion than many of the village's adults. This time, however, I didn't look forward to her company. My thoughts swirled with the desire to keep the truth from her and the ever-growing assurance that I could not.

The sun was low in the sky as Eliza and I walked across the yard hand in hand. She was quiet, as usual, but I could feel her excited anticipation of a night at the cottage. As soon as we entered the house, we found Holmes looking at scuff marks under the stairs, and I recalled that I hadn't considered his feelings on the matter of having the child stay with us.

"I see you're to come back to the village with us," he said promptly, addressing Eliza, who immediately let go of my hand and took his, staring at it and touching his long fingers one at a time. I didn't blame her; he had magnificent hands.

"Yes," I answered. "I decided that would be best."

"Indeed," said Holmes, but I couldn't tell from his face what he thought about it.

———

The police wagon was crowded on the way back to the village, but we were nearly silent. Chipping seemed afraid to say anything with the child present, for fear of upsetting her, and Holmes was in a world of his own. I held Eliza in my lap and let down a few strands of my hair for her to play with, and she seemed content.

Chipping left us at the cottage with a subdued goodbye, and Holmes swung Eliza down from the wagon, making her giggle and cling to his neck, which didn't seem to bother him. The case filled his mind, I could see, to the exclusion of almost everything else.

The child's delight was matched only by Mrs Turner's, and upon arrival at the house, the little girl was immediately taken from Holmes's arms along with her tiny suitcase to be settled into the second guest room and then plied with tea and as many pink frosted cakes as she could eat.

My friend and I took our familiar places on wing chair and sofa. "Holmes," I said. "I need your advice."

"You want to know how to tell the child that her father is dead, since her mother is in no condition to tell her, and she will no doubt hear from someone in the village if she is not told very quickly," he rejoined, and I realised that, as usual, he had not been as oblivious as he'd appeared.

"Exactly," I answered, looking down at my hands.

"I will do it," said Holmes, and my head jerked up.

"Are you sure?" I asked.

"Completely," he answered.

Part of me wanted to argue, but I had learned to trust Holmes, especially when he was as certain as he was about this. Besides, I truly had no idea how to break the news to her myself.

Dinner was a cheerful affair, with Eliza jabbering excitedly and Holmes proving that he could talk nonsense as well as anyone. I tried to join in, but a lump kept forming in my throat whenever I looked at the little girl. Finally, after we had all eaten our fill, Eliza began to realise that things were not as they usually were.

"Is mummy coming?" she asked, peering out the window into the darkness.

"No, love," I answered. "You're going to stay the night. Remember?" She pressed her face into my skirt then, and I looked over at Holmes for assistance, which he provided with his violin, playing a series of happy tunes that finally forced a grin out of the little girl. In the end, he was the one who ended the evening by asking Mrs Turner to get

Eliza ready for bed. The child looked stormy for a moment, as if she might balk, but Holmes lifted her chin with a single finger and promised to come and tell her a story, which filled her with curiosity.

"You don't intend to tell her right before she goes to sleep, do you?" I hissed as soon as she had tripped off with the housekeeper to be put into her nightdress.

"Certainly not," said Holmes with annoyance. "I shall tell her the story of Ali Baba and drag it out so long her body will be forced to give in to sleep."

I confess to sneaking into a shadowy recess across the hall to watch Holmes as he seated his spare frame on the end of Eliza's bed and went so far as to put out a long finger and tickle one of her small, pink feet, eliciting giggles.

"Hush, Madam," he said in a deep voice. "Keep still for the tale of *Ali Baba and the Forty Thieves*." Eliza's eyes widened, and she sat up against the pillow with rapt attention, clutching the much-loved Charles to her chest.

I don't know why it should have surprised me that Holmes was an excellent storyteller. He certainly had a large enough streak of the dramatic in him. His voice was by turns as quiet as a whisper and as loud as a thunderclap, and his fingers formed fleeing thieves and camels in the shadows on the wall. Eliza listened patiently, but I could see her eyelids beginning to droop after a while. My friend also noticed, and he made his voice quieter and his details more intricate, until the child's head rested on her pillow and he could make his exit without disturbing her.

"Come along," whispered Holmes, putting a light hand on my shoulder and propelling me into the sitting room. Of course he'd seen me watching, as I'd known he would.

"Marvellous performance," I said, once we were seated again.

"I hardly doubt you'd have done the same."

"Perhaps, but why did you do it? I don't suppose you're in the habit of telling bedtime stories to Dr Watson."

"Only if there's a case to be mulled over," said Holmes drily, leaning back in his chair and stretching his long legs. "I know, Irene, what it is like to lose one's parent."

"Oh," I said, unsure how to respond. I waited several long moments in the flickering light, but he did not continue.

"So do I," I ventured, though the silence had been so heavy that it seemed as if the previous comment had been uttered days before. "Both of my parents died during my first singing tour. I left a normal home, but there was nothing to return to when I came back." I didn't say this as bleakly as it sounds. Holmes and I had never spoken to each other about our distant pasts, and I found that I didn't mind revealing some of mine to him, though the intervening years and, hopefully, a measure of maturity, had lessened the sting of grief. Holmes nodded, but he did not reply.

After another long silence, I went to the kitchen to make tea and forestall the sleepiness that I could feel attempting to overtake me. Mrs Turner always went to bed early, and late-night tea was my one rebellion against her insistence on preparing all the food and drinks in the house herself. I did not know if Holmes wished to discuss the case, but I had no intention of going to bed without receiving an explanation of his thoughts.

When I returned with the tea tray, I found my friend looking through his notebook. "I hope your curiosity has not failed you to the point that you intend to go to bed without filling me full of questions like a Christmas goose," he teased, obviously aware of my intentions.

"I hope you're prepared," I rejoined, handing him a flowered teacup. I had purposefully selected the most hideously embellished one I owned in hopes of annoying him. It was, unaccountably, Mrs Turner's favourite.

"I believe," said Holmes after a few sips of the fragrant Darjeeling, "that we were finishing the discussion of the missing tobacco pouch."

"Yes," I said, casting my mind back.

"You will have realised, Irene, that the intentional removal of the man's tobacco pouch would have been a very strange move for a murderer to make. If the killer had wished to make it look like Phillimore had left of his own volition, then taking more than a tobacco pouch would have been the logical action. Edith, too, struck me as far too intelligent to have failed to notice the object's absence if she wasn't expecting it. That, coupled with the odd incident of the rabbit, began to suggest a chain of events to me."

"I don't suppose you intend to reveal it yet," I said, resigned to the wait.

"One must not guess, Miss Adler," he said, "and I was at the time unsure."

"Very well," I groused, not really irritated.

"The timing of the rabbit's sudden appearance, as I said before, surprised me, though I had expected it to be returned at some juncture. The material point is how much Edith Phillimore did not want me to look at it. I had already observed a certain amount of resistance in her to my taking the case at all. She purported to be pleased, but her demeanor told a different tale. Strange behaviour from a woman who was supposedly longing for her husband's return and had no particular reason to dislike me."

"At the house, too, she did not seem overly pleased with the idea of me poking about upstairs without her to guide me, though she took pains to act as if she didn't mind. Again, a peculiar way of behaving considering that the police have been over the place many times without uncovering anything. I could only attribute it to the fact that she had more faith in my powers of discovery than in the police's."

I rolled my eyes. "Very flattering. Do you think she killed him, then?"

"Certainly not," said Holmes. "All of this points to her not being the murderer."

"I don't quite follow," I admitted.

"Consider," said Holmes. "We have evidence that a missing man took his tobacco pouch with him when he disappeared, the one thing he could not be without because of his habit. His wife says nothing of this to the police, who are too focused on the presence of the man's clothing and umbrella to notice where something as small as a tobacco pouch ought to be. At the same time, a little girl's white rabbit goes missing and reappears without an explanation. No doubt, had we not been present, the mother would have passed it off as a child's forgetfulness. Finally, we have Edith Phillimore's obvious shock at her husband's death."

"Yes," I murmured. "She was even more surprised than I would have expected. The duration of the time that James has been missing would have suggested a very real possibility of foul play to most people."

"Just so," said Holmes with satisfaction. "Therein is the key. As strange as it is to contemplate, the evidence points to Edith knowing where her husband was all along, or at least being aware that he intended to leave. His death, though, was apparently not part of the plan, whatever it might have been."

"Isn't that unbearably coincidental?" I asked.

"I don't care about coincidence if it's the only possibility," said Holmes. "The reason for the disappearance will very likely provide at least a beginning for the investigation of the murder, and will probably do much more than that."

"Do you intend to tell the police?" I asked.

"Tell them what?" asked Holmes, smiling. "That I suspect that the child's white rabbit was some sort of signal between husband and wife? That a little tobacco dust indicates that Edith Phillimore has been successfully deceiving them the entire time? I would hardly be believed, and anyway, I have no desire to involve Inspector Graves more than necessary."

"What is your prior acquaintance with him?" I asked, unable to restrain my curiosity.

"Unfortunately, he was a protégé of Inspector Lestrade. He took that venerable gentleman's side in a disagreement during a case several years ago, and his dislike was hardened by the fact that I turned out to be correct."

"Naturally," I rejoined archly.

"I had no idea he'd ended up in the country, but I see that his abilities haven't eclipsed his teacher's."

"At least Chipping is agreeable," I put in.

"Very," said Holmes, and I suspected that he was teasing me.

"What do you plan to do now?" I asked, thinking I could predict his answer.

"I'll tell Eliza in the morning, and then I think we must question her mother. It may be the only hope for finding the murderer, and the longer the trail has to go cold, the more difficult our task will be."

"I agree," I answered. "And Holmes—" I added as I rose to leave the room, "are you sure you want to tell Eliza yourself?"

"I am," answered my friend, showing no sign of going to bed.

"Why?"

Holmes stared at nothing. "Perhaps because she reminds me of Mycroft."

"What?" I stopped halfway down the hall and turned back to face him.

"Oh yes," he answered, "Mycroft was a very fanciful child." My last look at him before I went to bed found him smiling to himself.

She was fond of him, too, for he had a remarkable gentleness and courtesy in his dealings with women.

—The Adventure of the Dying Detective

Chapter 6: Holmes

Holmes didn't sleep, a usual occurrence when he was mulling over a case. This night, however, his mind was partially occupied by the little girl sleeping in the guest room next to his, the child with a mind so much like his older brother's. That was what unsettled him. Mycroft, even at Eliza's age, would have seen something. The question was how to tease information out of the mind of a seven-year-old to whom flower petals were as important as human beings.

At present, though, his task was to tell her that her father wasn't coming back. The detective didn't think about his childhood often, but now he let himself remember the day of his mother's death. He had been barely old enough to speak in full sentences, and Mycroft hadn't been much older than Eliza was. Strangely, he could hardly remember his own response, but he could recall with absolute clarity the horror on his brother's face when the second housemaid had told them. He had spent years trying to wish that moment away, not to bring his mother back, but to erase the look of helpless pain on Mycroft's face. Eliza was not his brother, but she had a similar mind, and he would do his best.

———

Eliza awoke early in the morning, and Mrs Turner dressed her for a walk outside, as Holmes had requested. He felt very old when he saw her emerge from the guest room with Charles tucked under her arm. She wasn't smiling. "Good morning, Miss Eliza," he said. She simply nodded.

The detective took the child's hand and led her out of the cottage and down the hill toward the village. The morning wind was chilly, and he bent down to make sure her coat was secured around her. She stared at him before touching his nose with her finger, ostensibly to see if it felt as pointy as it looked. "Where are we going?" she asked.

"To the Winking Tree," said Holmes, and he felt his hand suddenly tugged forward by the excited little girl. Hardly anyone was about and none of the shops were open at the early hour, for which Holmes was grateful. He listened to the crunch of leaves under his feet and felt the brisk air sting his cheek, all the while hoping he was not a fool for endeavoring to tell the child himself.

When they reached the large beech tree, Eliza sat down underneath it immediately, and Holmes joined her. She looked surprised, but he took his magnifying glass out of his coat pocket and gave it to her. She spent a happy ten minutes looking at everything in sight under the glass. Finally, Holmes held out his hand and took it back. "Eliza," he said, "do you know where your father is?"

"At home," she said promptly. With effort, Holmes did not show his surprise.

"When did you last see him?"

"I went to put Charles in bed for a nap, and Papa was on the carriage. He was sleeping, too. He didn't wake up."

"What did you do then?" asked Holmes evenly.

"I went and told Mummy, and she sent me away with Mrs Merriwether." Holmes leaned against the tree trunk, thinking.

"Eliza, your father wasn't asleep." The little girl turned toward the detective and looked at him with wide eyes.

"Was he dead?" Holmes nodded wordlessly. "My cat Tiger died," she continued, "so Papa bought Charles for me because he said Charles couldn't die."

"That's right," said Holmes, trying to ascertain where her mind was headed.

"When will Papa come back?"

"He's not coming back," said Holmes, feeling something thick in his chest and beginning to wish he hadn't undertaken his current task.

"Oh," said Eliza. "Is he still in Wonderland?"

Holmes thought about this for a moment before replying. "You can always keep him in Wonderland in your mind."

Eliza seemed satisfied with this, and she fell silent. The detective didn't try to rush her. After a while, she crept close and buried her face in his coat. He did not move to touch her, and she did not cry.

A long time later, the little girl stood up. "I'm hungry."

"Me too," said Holmes, and he realised that he was.

———

Breakfast was an odd affair, with Eliza showing no signs of her newfound knowledge except an unusually subdued demeanor and The Woman giving Holmes meaningful glances every few moments that betrayed her insatiable curiosity about what had transpired. Mercifully, Mrs Turner took Eliza away to help her fold laundry as soon as breakfast was over, which gave ample opportunity for the detective to join Irene in the sitting room and submit to her questioning.

"Well?" she hissed, keeping her voice low so as not to carry to the back of the cottage where Mrs Turner and Eliza were working.

"The task is complete," said Holmes simply, knowing he wouldn't get off so easily.

70

"How did she take it?"

"A seven-year-old child, however intelligent, can hardly be expected to fully understand the finality of death, but the material point is that she took it even better than I expected on account of already having a subconscious inkling that it was true."

"What in the world do you mean?" asked Irene, staring at the detective as if he'd turned purple.

"She found the body," he replied succinctly, watching his companion's face drain of colour as the sense of what he'd said reached her mind. "Her brain appears to have interpreted her father's lack of response as sleep, but I believe she knew something more serious had happened."

"Didn't she tell anyone?"

"Unless she's lying, which I can't quite credit, she told her mother, who bundled her off with the cook."

"And then what?"

"I'm not clairvoyant, Miss Adler, but it appears that Edith waited for someone to find the body accidentally. The other possibility is that she told Warren what had happened and arranged for him to find it, but after speaking to him, I don't believe so."

"You spoke to him?"

"He encountered me at the house yesterday and told me the story of finding the body purely by chance, which I believe is true. There is simply no indication that any of his actions would have benefitted him if he was the actual killer."

"I see. Are you confident that we may eliminate him as a potential suspect?"

"Nearly so. If things continue in the same way they're going now, I believe we'll find ourselves looking in another direction entirely."

"I suppose we'll have to question Edith now, though I confess I'm not looking forward to it."

"I, however, am," said Holmes, in the midst of lighting his pipe. "Her feelings notwithstanding, I'm ready to hear the truth about what she knows and am not inhibited by bonds of friendship. Perhaps you might prefer to miss the interview. I'd be happy to conduct it alone."

Irene was silent for a moment, as if she was considering the offer. "Very well," she finally said, "but I'll expect a full rendition of events." Holmes was slightly surprised at her easy acceptance, but he said nothing.

Mrs Turner brought Eliza back into the room then, and Holmes held out his hand. "Miss Eliza, would you like to go home?"

The little girl looked from the housekeeper to The Woman as if she was afraid of answering incorrectly. "I want to see Mummy," she said finally.

"And you shall," answered the detective, letting a smile reach the corners of his bright eyes.

———

Eliza was nearly silent on the ride to the farm, her tiny hands twisted into her green frock. Holmes didn't disturb her. He had been a quiet child himself, and he saw no reason to interrupt the little girl's process of thought. Children, he believed, were capable of far more logic and understanding than adults usually admitted.

Finally, when the farmhouse was nearly in sight, he heard the child's quiet voice. "If papa is dead, I won't see him any more." The assertion was decidedly a statement rather than a question. "Will they put him in the ground?"

"Yes," answered Holmes.

Eliza didn't speak again until they reached the house and Holmes swung her down from the wagon. "You are a nice, pointy man," she said seriously. "I like you."

"The impression is—mutual," said Holmes, caught off his guard. No matter how well he thought he understood the fairer sex, its members still had an almost infinite ability to surprise him.

He followed the child into the servants' entrance, where he found the cook in conversation with the housemaid. Mrs Merriwether gave him a frosty look. "Mrs Phillimore was about sick with worry when she woke up and didn't see the child."

The detective almost snorted, his private opinion being that her desperation probably had as much to do with worrying about what the child might say as it did with worry for her whereabouts. "I assume you informed her that Miss Adler was taking perfectly adequate care."

"I knew nothing of the sort," retorted the old lady. "Miss Adler is widely known to be almost *bohemian* in her habits." She spoke the word as if it was akin to insanity of some kind, and the watching housemaid's blue eyes seemed in danger of falling out of her head if she opened them any wider.

"Shocking," murmured the detective, sounding as if he meant the opposite. "I wonder, then, that you let her go so easily yesterday. As you see, the child returns in good health. Where is her mother? I would like to deliver her back personally."

"That's not possible," snapped the cook. "She still hasn't left her room."

"Nevertheless," said Holmes coolly, "I believe she will see me. Please inform her of my presence."

Mrs Merriwether stared at him a moment as if trying to ascertain her likelihood of winning a battle of wills, but she finally nodded curtly to the diminutive maid. "Lewis, go and ask if Mrs Phillimore wishes to see this man."

The girl looked confused for a moment. "The name is Sherlock Holmes," the detective reminded her, trying to put her at her ease. It was obvious the cook wouldn't be won over to his side, so he determined to cultivate a positive relationship with the younger girl in case the association might prove useful later.

Eliza followed the housemaid upstairs, leaving Holmes alone with Mrs Merriwether, who showed her disdain by returning to her task of preparing vegetables as if the detective were not present, which suited him very well. Watson, he thought, would have been of great use in the present circumstance. He had a way with females in households everywhere that was unequalled by anyone else the detective had ever known.

After a few moments, the housemaid returned, standing in front of Holmes with a look of official purpose about her. "Mrs Phillimore says that if you please to wait downstairs, she will see you." The look the cook gave him was filled with malevolence.

The detective followed the girl into the parlour and took his seat on one of the uncomfortable chairs. He was not surprised that Edith desired to see him in a formal setting. She was obviously an intelligent woman, intelligent enough to have realised that he was likely to have some idea of her subterfuge. The cold formality of the parlour would afford her, he thought, a stronger feeling of confidence than would a more intimate setting.

The woman who joined him ten minutes later was pale and self-contained, though there was a desperation in her eyes that the detective hadn't seen there before. He rose and smiled at her. "Good day, Mrs Phillimore. I'm sorry to importune you at a difficult time."

"I doubt it," she answered weakly. "I assume you have questions for me." She sat down opposite Holmes with resignation written in her every movement.

If I had been less cautious I might have been more wise, but I was half crazy with fear that you should learn the truth.

—The Adventure of the Yellow Face

Chapter 7: Irene

As soon as Holmes and the child had left for the farm, I made ready for my intended tasks. Perhaps it was petty of me, but I relished knowing that I had been able to conceal from Holmes my wish to make an investigation of my own. I dressed in one of my finer frocks and prepared to visit the home of Charles Stevenson, barrister, and his wife, Jane.

The Stevenson home was on the coastal edge of the village, one of those houses that looks as if it would be bad tempered if it could speak. It was large and white and ugly and undoubtedly worth a great deal. I didn't look forward to entering it for the second time in my life, but I was determined to find out why Charles Stevenson had been in the Phillimore farmhouse on the day of the murder and if his presence had been a result of the discovery of the body or something prior to it. I couldn't get him out of my mind; the idea of a man like him coming to discuss business with a woman seemed hard to credit. Perhaps it was an insignificant detail, but I didn't like to leave anything unexplained.

I put on my most simpering smile and tucked a wisp of hair behind my ear—small ears are not always an advantage when one wishes to keep one's hair under control—and made my way up the tree-lined path to the door. I could see a maid's face pressed against the window, and I expected to see her starched self in the doorway.

Instead, the tall, ornate door was opened by a large-boned, dark-haired girl with a determined chin. "Julia," I said, surprised, "I didn't expect to see you."

She smiled with a look of defiance in her eyes that I couldn't place; we had never been enemies. "Come in, Miss Adler, I'll tell Mother you've come."

"No need," I said suddenly, improvising. "I'm just as happy to visit with you." I did my best to look as though nothing was amiss in the world.

Julia nodded, though she did not smile, and told the maid to order tea. I followed her into a small breakfast room, thinking all the while about how I might ask her what she knew about her father's involvement with the Phillimore tragedy.

We sat down at a small table that was arrayed in a lace tablecloth of ridiculous intricacy and stared at one another. Julia's taciturnity was uncharacteristic, but I knew her to be direct, and I made a decision to be the same. With her mother, I would have been far more subtle, but I knew the daughter to be boldly honest.

"I came to find out why your father was at the Phillimore house yesterday," I said. "You have heard, I am sure, that Sherlock Holmes of London is currently my guest, and his intent in being here is to unravel the James Phillimore case. I simply wish to know when your father arrived at the house."

Julia turned as white as the lace tablecloth, and the hand that held her teacup shook. For a moment, I was afraid she might faint. Her discomfiture shocked me and sent my thoughts into a whirlwind. Of all possible scenarios, this was certainly not one I had anticipated. For a moment, I wondered stupidly if she might have misheard my question, but I had spoken clearly.

"I—I don't know," she finally stuttered out. "My father isn't here, and my mother wouldn't know either. I'm afraid I can't help you."

It's not to my credit to admit that I accepted her answer, but my amazement at her response had disturbed me to the point that I let her usher me out before the tea had even been brought. I walked home without realising where my feet were taking me, lost in an attempt to figure out what had just happened.

Once I was alone, I thought through events. Julia's presence at her parents' home wasn't unusual in itself; a new bride living near her parents has every right to visit them. At the same time, her relationship with her father was widely known to be strained, ever since he'd tried to prevent her marriage with Edward Rayburn. The fact that he had eventually relented had not, apparently, healed the breach. Of course, I reasoned, no one knew of any bad blood between Julia and her mother, which could account for her visit.

Her reaction to my question was another matter entirely. I'd fully expected her to say she knew nothing of the matter at all. Barring that, I'd anticipated a mundanely businesslike answer relating to her father's professional capacity. What I had certainly not expected was an emotional reaction, particularly one as extreme as she had expressed. Clearly, it pointed to something, and I determined to puzzle it out while drinking a pot of tea.

I found Mrs Turner darning socks, a pastime she enjoyed to an extent I could not fathom. She looked up with a certain kind of disapproval when I entered, a look that I had learned meant she was pleased to see me. I smiled. "I've just finished a most unaccountable social call," I said, "and I need tea to help me think it over." This appeal was successful in its blatant attempt to move the heart of my housekeeper, and she rose majestically and went into the kitchen. I knew, to my delight, that a pot of tea also meant an array of biscuits and cakes.

I sat down at the table with a few sheets of notepaper. At the top of the first sheet, I wrote, "Julia Rayburn Problem," but before I got any further, I heard someone at the door. After the excitement of the previous two days, I felt I was prepared for anyone to be standing in my doorway. I was wrong.

The form that greeted me was that of none other than Edward Rayburn. He took his hat off and stared at me uncertainly, as though I might bite.

"Please come in, Mr Rayburn," I said, taking pains to conceal my considerable surprise. "It's a pleasure to see you."

The young man followed me like a large puppy and sat on the edge of the sofa as if he was afraid of soiling it. My unflappable housekeeper immediately materialised with two teacups instead of one and a variety of edibles which would have satisfied eight people as well as two.

Edward held his teacup gingerly, as if it might come alive in his hand, then cleared his throat and blurted out, "Miss Adler, my mum was a midwife."

"Yes—I know," I answered, slightly shocked. I didn't mind the discussion of such things, but they were usually far from the lips of the villagers, especially men.

"It is—I mean, when I was a little boy, she used to take me on her rounds with her. I wouldn't be in the room, you understand, but I knew what went on."

"Very proper, I'm sure," I said, trying to encourage his halting narrative.

"The thing is, I think Julia—is—" He couldn't continue. I waited for a moment, but it was obvious that uttering the word in my presence was more than he could manage.

"You mean that Julia is going to have a baby?" I asked matter-of-factly, hoping that my tone would help to put him at his ease. He nodded, blushing red to the tips of his large ears.

"I didn't know who else to talk to, Miss Adler. It's—you know, it's too soon for that with us, at least for—for any of the signs. I didn't want to believe it, but it's getting more and more obvious."

"You came to me because you know my past reputation," I said.

"It wasn't just that," he answered, raising his head and looking at me with clear green eyes. "Julia likes you. She doesn't like many people around here, but she likes you."

"I see. You understand what this means if it's true," I continued.

"I do," he answered.

"What will you do? You'd have reason to leave her."

Edward fixed me with a steady gaze. "You're quite mistaken, Miss Adler, if you think I'd ever do that."

"What?" I'm afraid I looked at him as if he had lost his mind.

"My feelings have not changed," he said simply.

"I don't like the idea of you as a martyr," I returned with equal directness.

He laughed, and his face transformed into a boy's. "I'm much too happy to be a martyr. Julia is the best company I've ever had. I can't do without her."

"You don't mind?" I asked, still unable to comprehend his position.

"Yes," he said, "but all the minding I've done has only reminded me of how much I care for her. I know that she did not always care for me, but I believe she does now."

"I cannot argue with you," I said, "though I urge you to consider your position."

He smiled again. "I used to wonder what I could possibly do for her, how a farmer could ever give anything to a woman like her. Now I have something to give, and it's mine alone."

"What would you like me to do?" I asked.

"I want to know if I'm right," he said, "from her own mouth. I can't ask her, but I believe she would tell you. I don't want to hear it from someone else. I just—want her to tell me herself. I would forgive her if she would just tell me."

I paused before answering. "Very well. I will do what I can." He left then, and I sat alone in my house for a long time. I had little doubt that Rayburn's suspicion was correct. He wasn't a stupid man, and he adored Julia. That, coupled with her strange behaviour, made me think that he was not likely to be mistaken.

I did not claim a position of moral superiority, but my sensibilities revolted from the idea that Julia had married the farmer simply for his name or the status of marriage. Had she thought he was stupid enough to accept a child as his own without question, even if the timing was wrong? Of course, most men did not have Rayburn's knowledge of the first signs of pregnancy. That was the curse of irony, it seemed. Julia had married the one man in Fulworth most likely to figure out her situation.

Mrs Turner brought lunch to me after a while, but I didn't eat. For once, knowing what I needed to do chased away my appetite completely. I didn't want to speak to

82

Julia, didn't want to be part of a something between a man and his wife. But there was something in Edward's manner that wouldn't let go of me. He was, I thought, a good man. I had known very few of those in my life. I had known plenty of women in trouble similar to Julia's, victims of men with hearts as small as Edward Rayburn's was vast. As much as I sympathised with whatever might have led to Julia's circumstances, though, I could not condone the use of a good man by a woman who simply needed his name. And yet—I had seen the look of love in Julia's eyes when she watched her husband. I had observed the way she spoke to him and watched her smile when he took her hand, small moments when she thought no one else was paying attention. Given what I had seen, I would never have doubted her affection, and I still found it difficult to do so. I didn't know what to think. Truthfully, I wished for Holmes, to be able to explain the situation to him and hear his assessment. Unfortunately, he was at the farm, and in any case, his presence was not conducive to the task I had agreed to undertake for Edward

I was beginning to feel as if I were in some strange, enchanted state in which everywhere I visited must be visited again and again—first the Phillimore farm and now the Stevenson house, where I expected Julia to have remained. I didn't let myself speculate about what I would find when I arrived. A great many of Holmes's opinions were not shared by me, but I found his revulsion to guessing extremely reasonable. I could not manage to be as religious as he was about eradicating the practise altogether, but in the present circumstance, I forced my mind to focus on other topics. If Julia was pregnant, the ramifications would be ample, but since I could not yet know, I filled my walk to the house with thoughts about the Phillimore case and the things I knew of it, though they did not seem a great many when I'd added them all up in my mind. I hoped Holmes might have something of value to add when he returned.

But the deception could not be kept up forever.

—A Case of Identity

Chapter 8: Holmes

Holmes looked at the pale woman opposite him, and he saw neither a cold-blooded killer nor a greedy swindler. "Perhaps it will be easier for you if I begin with what I know," he said.

"Very well," she answered listlessly.

"Some time before the wedding of Julia Stevenson and Edward Rayburn, your husband got into some sort of trouble, serious enough for him to consider fleeing Fulworth. You decided to stage his disappearance as a mystery, so that whomever he felt threatened by would think that there was no hope of finding out his whereabouts from you. Not wishing, I suspect, to disrupt a wedding, you waited until after the ceremony had concluded to deliver your shocking news. The police were called, but you had been careful, and they did not find any clue to your husband's whereabouts." While the detective spoke, Edith's face remained impassive.

"The importance of Eliza's rabbit took me a little while to puzzle out, but I determined that he was a signal between you and your husband. Once you had played your part and alerted the village to James's disappearance, you posted it to him, mailing it to a predetermined location. In return, your husband posted it back to you to confirm that he had reached his destination without issue. I assume a servant was used to post and retrieve it so that it could be placed in a way that made it seem as if Eliza had simply misplaced her toy."

"I began to suspect all of this when I perceived your distaste for my presence and your strong reaction to my interest in Eliza's rabbit. You had fooled the police, but you did not fool me, as I think you realised."

"When do you intend to tell the police?" asked Edith, defeat in her voice.

Holmes drilled her with his eyes. "As you have probably ascertained, if I told them this, they would immediately believe they had found the murderer—a wife with knowledge of her husband's whereabouts that no one else had, who stood to do quite well if he died. This is why I do not intend to tell them anything until I have discovered the murderer."

"You don't believe I'm guilty?"

"Of deceit, yes. Of murder, no. If you wish the real murderer to be found, however, you must tell me the entire truth about your husband's flight."

"Very well." Edith looked away from Holmes then, clenching her hands as if she were a nervous child. "Six weeks ago, my husband started acting strangely. You will have heard that he is—was—not a sociable man, but he became even less so than usual. He hardly spoke, and he seemed absent, as if he were with me in body but not in spirit."

"After a week, I asked him what was wrong. He— had never acted to me the way he acted to everyone else. I had always been his confidante, so I could not understand his newfound reticence. He wouldn't answer at first, but finally he told me the truth: He was being blackmailed."

"By whom?"

"You may have seen the doctor who was here yesterday—Dr Clarke from the village. He blackmailed my husband in several letters."

"May I see them?"

"I'm afraid not. James took them with him. They haven't been found. I never saw them. James was too ashamed to show them to me." Holmes let out a nearly imperceptible huff of frustration.

"What was the matter of the blackmail?"

"I suppose it doesn't matter now. Dr Clarke has been the family physician since before my husband was born. He threatened to reveal that James's real mother was the family's housemaid, who died several years ago."

"A fact that had been known to your husband?"

"No, he'd never known until he received the first letter."

"And what was the doctor hoping to gain?"

"Money. James never told me how much, but he paid him regularly for a while. There was no proof of what he said, of course, but my husband couldn't bear the thought of having the whole village wonder about his father and drag the family's name through the mud. He hated being singled out."

"But why now?"

"James said it was because Dr Clarke had speculated and was trying to glean money from whatever possible quarters he could."

"I see," said the detective. "What led to the disappearance?"

"After I had finally convinced James to tell me what was troubling him, he also told me that things could not continue as they were, or we would be unable to pay. I tried to convince him to go to the police, but he, I'm afraid, had given up. Dr Clarke is a powerful and respected man."

"James began to insist that he couldn't stay in Fulworth. I begged him to reconsider, but he believed that his position was untenable here. What he hoped was to leave and bring Eliza and me to join him later, taking care of selling the farm from afar and anonymously. You may—you may, Mr Holmes, think that my husband's actions were extreme, but you didn't know him. He valued his pride very, very highly, and he'd always felt that as a farmer, he could never match the power of men like the doctor."

"Please continue with the specifics of the plan," said Holmes, beginning to tire of the subjective aspects of the narrative.

"It was as you said. We determined that James would leave on the day of the wedding so that I could reveal his disappearance in a place where the whole village could hear of it, including the doctor. He went back inside for his umbrella and hid in the cellar until the property was clear of people so that it would seem as if he'd simply vanished. Once the police investigation was concluded, I was to depart the village with my little girl and meet him, leaving the farm in the hands of Warren and the other farmhands until it could be quietly sold. I didn't know precisely where he intended to settle, but he was to write and tell me in a few weeks. The return of Eliza's rabbit was assurance that all was proceeding smoothly—until yesterday." Edith's voice faltered, and she ceased speaking for a moment. "I—didn't expect to never see him again, you know. It's like he really disappeared, Mr Holmes. My husband went back into the house, and all that's left is his shell." She dabbed hard at her eyes for a moment.

"Who posted the rabbit?" asked Holmes.

"The cook, Mrs Merriwether," Edith replied. "I think she would kill for me." After she realised what she'd said, she shook her head sharply. "I didn't mean that."

"I didn't expect so," said Holmes. "I had already observed her loyalty to you."

"Do you know the vicinity of your husband's destination?"

"That's the problem," said Edith. "I don't know. The rabbit was sent to a specific address in London, where my husband's cousin resides, but James didn't plan to stay there. I thought—I thought he was somewhere else in London, but I have no idea where."

"I believe you," said the detective. "Now, Mrs Phillimore, have you any idea who might have killed your husband? Did anyone other than the cook know of the plan?"

"No," said Edith, "and even she didn't know the particulars. She refused to let me tell them to her. I thought of the doctor, but I don't know what he would have gained by killing a man who had been paying him regularly."

"No," said Holmes. The detective rose. "Thank you for your help, Mrs Phillimore. I will do my best to put an end to this mystery."

The widow half smiled. "It's ironic, Mr Holmes, but now I'm actually thankful to have you on the case."

"Understandable," he said, turning to leave, but Edith stopped him with a hand on his arm.

"I should thank you for being kind to Eliza. When I awoke, I was scared to death she'd found out about James by more difficult means. I'm so very glad she learned the truth from friends."

"I'm glad you consider me a friend in this matter, Mrs Phillimore," was all Holmes answered.

Holmes found the small maid beating rugs outside the farmhouse. "Miss Lewis," he said, which turned her face red from the politeness of it, "do you know where I might find Dr Clarke from the village?"

"You know the Winking Tree on the green?"

"Yes."

"Go beyond it to the big, ugly houses down the lane. His is the plainest one. Be careful he don't dose you with something."

"Thank you," said Holmes, smiling to himself as he took his leave.

———

The housemaid, the detective soon realised, was not incorrect in her observation. The wealthiest members of Fulworth society had a row of houses that skirted the village, as if they were too rich to quite allow themselves to be a part of daily life, but too fond of recognition to be entirely out of it, either. One house, however, was noticeably plainer than the others, as if its size was for function rather than form. To this home the detective went, and he was met at the door by a solidly-built, middle-aged woman—Mrs Parkfield, the doctor's assistant.

"Dr Clarke isn't seeing patients today," she said stiffly.

"I am not a patient," said Holmes. "I wish to see him about the Phillimore murder."

Without another word, the woman turned and disappeared into the house, her black skirt swooshing around her as if it was trying hard to keep up with its wearer. Holmes looked around him, and he understood the impression of functionality that seemed to pervade even the exterior of the house, for its front, at least, was furnished as a doctor's surgery more than a home.

The woman in black returned after a few moments, and she motioned to Holmes. "Dr Clarke will see you in his study," she said, already starting down a wide hallway. The detective followed, lengthening his strides to keep up with her brisk pace.

She led him to a large, book-lined room. "Here he is," she said tersely, leaving Holmes just inside the door, facing a huge wooden desk at which was seated the elderly form of Dr Isaac Clarke.

"Good day, young Holmes," he said.

"Doctor," said the detective, taking his seat in a chair in front of the old man.

"I count that it has been above thirty years since I last laid eyes on you."

"Quite right," said Holmes. "When we last met, you were simply Clarke, a young man trying his hand as a doctor's assistant."

"I'm still simply Clarke," said the doctor with a sardonic smile, "though hardly young any more. I knew you at Oakhill Farm, but I thought you might prefer not to be recognised while you were acting in your professional capacity."

"I appreciate your discretion, though even now, I am acting in my professional capacity. I have heard a story today, and I wish to hear your explanation of it."

"Indeed?" said the doctor, leaning back in his large chair.

"In short," said Holmes, "Edith Phillimore claims that you blackmailed her husband into disappearing."

"What?" The doctor sat forward in his chair and pushed his palms down on his desk forcefully. "What sort of motivation could have driven me to do such a thing?"

"Money," said Holmes simply. "I would not suggest such a thing if I could avoid doing so."

"Believe me," said the old man with heightened colour, "it is only fondness for the boy you once were that is keeping you in this house at this moment."

"Very well," said the detective, unperturbed. "The widow claims that you extorted money from her husband by threatening to expose that he was the child of his father's indiscretion with a household servant."

The doctor's face suddenly changed, and he threw back his head and laughed. "I don't mean to be irreverent about a man's death, Holmes, but Edith Phillimore is having you on or has been deceived herself. Robert Phillimore was as pure as the driven snow. I wasn't the doctor who attended the birth. I confirmed Mrs Phillimore's pregnancy, but she gave birth elsewhere, at her sister's home in London. The family had three servants, all of whom were at home at the time. I am hardly the only person still living who was alive and would recall that no one in the household was with child except Louise Phillimore."

"Thank you," said Holmes. "I suspected this, but I am glad to hear your confirmation. The story the widow told me was deeply flawed, but I did not wish to dismiss the possibility until I had spoken to you."

"Since you're not likely to get much out of Graves, I should tell you that Phillimore had been dead for some time when he was found, several hours at least. His corpse showed signs of being dragged before it was placed in the carriage house. Here are my notes, if you care to see them." The elderly doctor handed Holmes a stack of pages written in his spidery hand.

"Thank you," said the detective. "Edith Phillimore knew that her husband planned to disappear. The question now is what happened to cleave soul and body in the mean time, causing him to never be seen alive again. I will take my leave to ponder the question."

"Humour an old man and stay for tea—or perhaps something stronger," said Clarke, smiling. "Since my dear wife's death, I welcome rational company. I experience it so rarely."

"Not today," said Holmes, "but I promise to return before I leave the village."

"Don't forget that I used to let you read my books."

"Certainly not," said the detective, smiling.

There is nothing new under the sun. It has all been done before.

—A Study in Scarlet

Chapter 9: Irene

"Hello, Julia," I said when she again opened the door of her parents' home. I had been afraid she might try to keep me out, but she ushered me in with a quizzical expression.

"If you wish to speak to my mother," she said softly, "I might be able to fetch her for you."

"On the contrary," I said, "I am here to speak to you."

"Whatever for?" she asked, making no effort to seat me, but continuing to stand over me awkwardly in the opulent front hallway of the house.

"Your husband came to see me," I said bluntly, hoping to shock her into a response.

"I see," she answered, her face betraying nothing whatsoever. "Shall we walk outside?" I nodded, and she led the way out to the lane and away from the village. I respected her silence for several minutes and let myself enjoy the pleasure of being outdoors, but the sky began to turn grey, and I knew that rain was not far away.

"Come to my house," I said, and Julia followed absently, as if her mind was entirely elsewhere. Had I not recognised the coming rain myself, I believe she would have stayed out in it and hardly noticed.

As it was, we reached my cottage just as the first fat drops began to make their acquaintance with the ground. I installed Julia on the sofa with one of Mrs Turner's afghans and took my seat in Holmes's wing chair, which seemed oddly appropriate under the circumstances.

"Julia," I finally ventured, "I can't think of an easier way to go about this. Your husband came to see me because he had a question that he didn't want to ask you himself, but I have one that I'd like to ask first: Do you love him?"

The girl didn't look up. Instead, she twisted one finger through a lock of her black hair and fidgeted with her other hand, staring hard at the lace pattern in the afghan on her lap. "I do love him," she finally said, and the sudden intensity in her voice surprised me. "I wish I didn't, but I do."

"You know," I said gently, "that his mother was a midwife."

"Yes," she answered, and the colour drained from her face. "You don't mean he—"

"He's not a stupid man," I said evenly, watching her. "He knows the signs, without even trying."

What little doubt I'd had of the truth of Edward's claim was immediately dispelled by the sob that burst from his wife's throat. Julia put her hands in front of her face and leaned forward, weeping into her lap. I moved to sit beside her and put an arm around her shoulders the way Mrs Turner had used to do for me when dark memories clouded my first months in Fulworth.

As the distraught girl began to calm, my mind made a leap of intuition of which Holmes would not have approved. Or, perhaps, he would have said that my subconscious mind had somehow assimilated evidence that pointed where my conscious mind finally led me.

"Julia," I said, "James Phillimore was the father of your child, wasn't he?" In that moment, I knew what Holmes must feel when he revealed a deduction that held monumental power over someone's very life.

Julia's voice faltered, "Yes, that's true."

"I believe I know what happened," I said. "Will it be easier for you if I suggest events? You may correct me if I'm wrong in particulars."

She nodded. "Please."

97

"Last year, you returned home from school. You had left Fulworth as a child, but you returned as a woman, in appearance if not in wisdom and experience. Somehow— perhaps at church or a village fete, you met a farmer."

"The Harvest Festival," she murmured. "He was showing flowers."

"I won't claim to know exactly what happened," I said, "but believe me, I understand more than you could possibly realise. He asked for things, and you gave them. I think that you were not forced, but your naïveté was exploited." She looked as if she might disagree, but she said nothing.

"He had a wife, but he said he didn't love her, and you believed him."

"No," she said suddenly. "He told me that he loved her very much, but that he loved me even more. That is why I gave him what he asked for."

"The two of you were discreet," I continued, "and nothing disturbed you for a few months."

"Except conscience," Julia muttered, almost to herself.

"Then the worst thing of all—you were pregnant."

I stopped speaking, and Julia continued instead. "I didn't want to believe it, but I finally knew that it must be so. I didn't go to the midwife; I knew my shame would be all over the village."

"I expect you're wondering where poor Edward comes into it. He's always been in love with me. Before we were ten years old, we used to plan our life together. He was heartbroken when my parents sent me away to school, and when I came back, he asked to court me. I declined several times. James Phillimore was a mystery and a prize. Edward had always been available whether I wanted him or not."

"After I knew the baby was coming, I wrestled with myself. Edward, I knew, would come the moment I called him. His name and standing were a way out of my difficulty. Other women in the village have given birth before their times, and I knew that Edward would propose very quickly if I would let him. I could, I thought, make it seem that the child was his, and if any tongues wagged in the village, they would think that any indiscretion had occurred between a couple who were now married. With luck, however, I planned to pass it off as a premature birth."

"You may not believe me, but I could hardly bear to do it. I had a sister's affection for Edward that was left over from childhood, but it became even worse than that. As we began to court, I finally understood what kind of man he was. I saw him with new eyes. Phillimore could be cold and even cruel, but Edward was kind and gentle. He respected me as James never did. The regret, you may imagine, was excruciating, as I realised what I had given up for a few occasional moments with a man who had never truly loved me."

"Phillimore took monstrous advantage of you. Where was he when all of this was occurring?"

"He never saw me again after I knew about the baby. He said it would be better for me not to be seen with him. The only promise he made was that he would leave the village."

"Better for you, my eye," I snorted.

"I know that now," she said, "but it was like he'd cast a spell on me. I can see why Edith married him. He could be very, very charming in a mysterious way, as if you might just come to know him if you stayed around a moment longer, but the right moment never came, and he never gave anything of himself."

99

"I understand," I said, meaning it.

"I'll have to leave Edward, of course," she faltered. "He's far too lovely a man to be chained to a woman like me."

"He is a good man," I agreed, "but there's no need for you to be a martyr. He's willing to forgive."

"I don't care," said Julia. "I'd no right to try to trap him this way. Even if he hadn't figured it out, I don't think I could have managed to go through with it. At least, Miss Adler, you can think that much good of me."

"Believe me," I answered, "I'm not claiming any sort of superiority. I know that my past is a rumour in the village, and believe it or not, the truth is more sensational than the whispers."

"Really?" Julia looked slightly incredulous. "I'd always assumed it was just because you're a bit—unusual and unmarried and American."

"I am all those things," I said, "and I'm a widow, but I've also been a thief and other less mentionable things. You should ask Mr Holmes about it some time."

"What about your Mr Holmes?" she asked, half smiling for the first time since she'd entered my house.

"Holmes," I said, "is as the Bible says: The same yesterday, today, and forever."

"There's a great deal to be said in favour of that," Julia mused, unconsciously touching her belly. "Ed thinks I'm spending the night at my mother's," she continued. "Tomorrow I'll figure out where I'm to go."

"Must you be so hasty?" I asked. "Can't you give your husband a chance to prove his love?"

"He's already borne far too much," she said resignedly.

"Phillimore is at least as responsible as you are, and in my eyes, much more," I said, trying again.

"I don't dispute that," she said, "but I'm the one who duped Edward into giving me his name."

"True," I said, "but now that he knows, he gives it willingly." I hesitated for a moment. "Julia, I am more than ten years older than you are, and I know how rare men like Edward Rayburn are in this world."

"Do you also know what it's like to contemplate incurring a debt to someone that can never possibly be repaid?" she asked bitterly.

"Yes," I answered, looking around at the home Holmes had given me, "I do."

Julia rose then, and she left the cottage without another word, walking home to her mother through the afternoon rain.

———

I did not notice when Holmes entered the house, so deep was I in thought. He took his place opposite me on the sofa. "I see that Rayburn paid you a visit. His boots left traces of a peculiarly-coloured clay that is only found in the part of the county where his farm is situated."

"Yes," I said, "both he and his wife came to see me, but separately."

"I see," said my friend. "Had these visits anything to do with the case?"

"I don't know yet," I answered. "Edward came to tell me that he suspected his wife was pregnant with the child of another man, and Julia corroborated his suspicion."

"Indeed," said Holmes. "Was Rayburn asking for help to extricate himself?"

"No, he doesn't want help," I said quietly, looking out the window into the falling dusk.

"As I would have expected, from what you said of his character before," said my companion, lighting his pipe with long, steady fingers.

"I did not," I replied.

"Perhaps you credit the fairer sex with a better-developed ability to forgive."

"Or perhaps I think us undeserving of such profligate kindness," I retorted, a trifle bitterly.

"Kindness is far from profligate when it is bestowed on the object of one's regard," said Holmes quietly. I stopped myself before I asked him how he knew.

I have not lived for years with Sherlock Holmes for nothing.

—The Hound of the Baskervilles

Chapter 10: Holmes

The detective watched his companion carefully. He had learned that like Watson's, but unlike his own, her moods were subject to change based on the fluctuations of a case and the information she uncovered. He sometimes wondered what it would be like to inhabit such a mercurial existence, to be at the mercy of whatever one happened to discover. He did not relish the idea.

"I take it, by your obvious eagerness to tell me more, that these encounters of your afternoon somehow potentially relate to the Phillimore case, as opposed to simply being a tangle of human affections in the common way," he finally said.

"Yes," The Woman answered, twining her fingers together. "I've something to tell you that may change things considerably. When you left today, my intention was to ascertain why Julia's father, Charles Stevenson, was present at the examination of Phillimore's body. I found Julia at her parents' home, and her reaction to my question was so strong as to be bizarre. I have since learned from her visit and her husband's the reason for her behaviour, but it relates to our investigation much more than I'd realised."

Irene took a deep breath, as if for dramatic emphasis. "James Phillimore was the father of Julia's child."

"Indeed," said Holmes, not begrudging The Woman her moment of triumph. "That puts certain discoveries of mine in their proper places."

"Yes?" she said, leaning forward.

"Edith Phillimore was as forthright as I expected once she knew she had been found out. She readily corroborated the fact that Charles the rabbit was a messenger between her and her husband. She also told me the reason for her husband's flight, the fact that he had been blackmailed by Dr Clarke."

"I can't believe that," said Irene immediately.

"Your skepticism is to your credit in this case," said the detective. "Fortunately, I have known Dr Clarke for many years, and I found the idea of him extorting money based on a rumour about someone's illegitimate origins beyond credibility. I went to see him, and he put the idea to rest."

"So Edith was lying once again?" said Irene, incredulous.

"No, I think not," said Holmes. "I believe she herself was deceived by her husband."

"That certainly harmonises with the picture of his character that Julia provided," Irene added.

"After hearing your additions to the story," the detective continued, "I believe that Phillimore was desperate after finding out about Julia's pregnancy and concocted a story to convince his wife to help him disappear. We have no way of knowing if he ever actually intended for his wife and child to join him."

"Disgusting," said The Woman, repugnance written all over her beautiful face.

"Quite," said Holmes, "though he does seem to have had real affection for Eliza."

"What does this mean for the case?" asked Irene after a moment of silence.

Instead of answering, the detective went to the door of the cottage. "I hear footsteps approaching," he said.

"Mrs Turner should be returning from the shops now," said Irene.

"No," said the detective, "the footfall is heavier."

"Why not open the door and see which of us is correct?" said The Woman, slightly exasperated. Holmes did so, and a burst of wet wind entered the house, along with a ruddy man wearing a luxurious moustache.

"Hello, Holmes and Miss Adler," said Watson, and he looked past his friend to nod to Irene, who had risen and was surveying both men with surprise.

"Welcome, Dr Watson. I'm sorry we didn't anticipate your arrival," she answered.

"It's no matter," said the doctor, "I suppose my telegram didn't make it to you."

"I'm afraid not," she answered. "The office in the village is not always reliable."

"Then please accept my apology for my importunate arrival," answered Watson gallantly. "Miss Willow," he added, looking up at his tall flatmate, "has eloped with a curate. I certainly hope it was fully her own doing and not assisted by the machinations of anyone else."

"Your implication does me dishonour," Holmes answered, but he could hear The Woman inelegantly smothering a laugh in the background.

"Please do settle in, and I'll make a pot of tea," she said, gliding into the kitchen and leaving the two men alone. Watson took his small suitcase and black doctor's bag into the guest room next to his friend's, then rejoined Holmes in the sitting room.

"I'm glad you've come, Watson," said the detective, relaxing on his winged throne. "I've grown so accustomed to your ever-faithful presence that I find your absence more inconvenient than ever."

Watson smiled. "And I, I'll admit, find London dreadfully dull without a case to keep me occupied. I'm afraid you've acclimated me to your ways, old friend. How is the Phillimore disappearance progressing?"

"As often happens," Holmes answered, "the disappearance has become a murder. The interesting feature of this particular case, however, is that a certain amount of proof exists that the disappearance happened significantly before the murder. In other words, the man did not disappear because he was murdered; rather, the murder took place at an as-yet-undetermined time afterward."

"I do," Holmes continued, "find myself in need of your particular speciality."

"What sort of speciality?" Watson asked curiously. "I have my revolver."

"Not that," the detective rejoined. "One of your more delicate specialties. I need you to worm your way into the heart, as it were, of the Phillimores' sour-tempered cook."

Watson huffed resignedly. "If you're certain. What sort of information are you seeking?" Holmes spent the next ten minutes giving his friend an overview of the case, a process that felt nearly as natural as breathing, so often had he done it.

Irene finally returned with a tray and sat down next to Watson on the sofa. "I confess, Holmes," she said, "that I am in the dark as to our next logical step."

"In general," the detective answered, "we must find the missing link between the murder and the association between James Phillimore and Julia Rayburn. There can hardly fail to be one. In particular, I wish to know what Mrs Merriwether knows, which friend Watson will find out for us."

"Do you want me to tell Edith that her husband was a philandering liar?" asked The Woman, spitting the words out with distaste.

"Soon," Holmes replied. "First things first; I wish to examine the notes made by Dr Clarke, who viewed the body right after it was found."

"You didn't view it yourself?" asked Watson incredulously.

"Unfortunately," said Holmes, "I was obstructed by the presence of an Inspector Graves, whom you may remember as an assistant to our friend Lestrade."

"Unpleasant," said Watson, wrinkling his nose.

"Nevertheless," said Holmes, "I have the doctor's notes, which are nearly as thorough as my own would have been."

"Goodness," said Irene, looking up from her teacup, "high praise indeed."

The detective looked at her coolly. "When I was a child, my parents sent me to Fulworth one summer to stay with a distant cousin. Dr Clarke, merely a medical assistant at the time, solved a highly sensational murder in Fulworth simply by viewing the corpse. I have rarely seen the equal of the performance. I read all his books that summer, hoping to absorb the ability."

"The osmosis appears to have been successful," answered The Woman, smiling.

"We share a certain similarity of mind," Holmes replied, momentarily transported back to his youth, but forcing himself to return to the present immediately.

For the next half hour, The Woman and the doctor conversed quietly while Holmes read the sheaf of papers given to him by Dr Clarke. He was well aware that if Clarke had been somehow involved in the murder, then his information would have been compromised. After seeing the old man, however, he was convinced that it was not so. Furthermore, in the few moments he'd had in the room with the corpse, while his attention appeared to be focused on the distasteful Inspector Graves, he'd actually had time to make a few deductions of his own, which the doctor's notes corroborated. That fact, coupled with the fact that he'd found Edith Phillimore's story of the doctor's involvement entirely preposterous, assured the detective that he could trust his old friend.

Sometime during Holmes's perusal, Mrs Turner arrived at the cottage laden with packages, which she nearly dropped upon beholding Watson. "Doctor," she stammered, "what a surprise. Miss Adler didn't inform me of your intention to visit, or I would have had something ready for you." She looked severely upon Irene, who grinned back with, Holmes thought, perverse amusement.

"Please don't trouble yourself," said Watson, rising and taking the housekeeper's hand. "Miss Adler didn't know herself. I'd intended to stay in town to fulfil certain obligations, but they have since disappeared, and here I am." Mrs Turner blushed and whisked away the tea tray Irene had produced, glaring down upon it as if she approved of neither its contents nor its arrangement.

"Sometimes," said Irene, "she reminds me a great deal of a girls' school headmistress."

"Or headmaster," said Watson. "I'll wager she could do battle with either of the ones I experienced."

"I love her for it," said Irene quietly, and Holmes saw a soft look come over her. He was glad. Uniting The Woman and the housekeeper had been his own doing, based on his knowledge of each. He had done well, he thought with satisfaction. Not all of his cases were large ones.

Sometimes he used his abilities in quieter ways, but he was no less satisfied when he succeeded.

That night, Watson and Mrs Turner went to bed before the detective and his hostess, as was the usual practise when the flatmates visited. Holmes was quiet, pondering the developments of the day and putting them into their proper places in his understanding of the case. From the evidence of his own trained eyes and Clarke's notes, he was fully convinced that Phillimore had been killed somewhere other than the Oakhill premises and then dragged there by a particularly vindictive murderer or, perhaps, a vindictive accomplice. The placement of the corpse atop the ancestral carriage seemed particularly brazen, the work of someone who was fully convinced that he or she could not be caught or else didn't care, instead wishing to make the strongest statement possible. It suggested a combination of hatred and an impression of power that intrigued Holmes and also perplexed him. As of yet, no one he'd considered had impressed him as having the proper temperament.

"Holmes, are you sure Edith is innocent?" asked Irene, breaking the silence after a very long time.

"Yes, I am," said Holmes, "though I have considered at length how she might still be a viable suspect. However, I find the idea even more difficult to entertain than that of Peter Warren as the killer. For one, her whereabouts can be accounted for at significant moments. For another, we know that Phillimore was not killed until after he'd run away; for Edith to have subsequently killed him and then displayed his body for all to see would have been madness, and she is not insane. The one thing I find incredible is her willingness to believe her husband's story of being blackmailed by Dr

Clarke without seeing the letters he'd supposedly sent or any other proof whatsoever."

"That part I comprehend," said The Woman, staring into her long-cold tea. "When my husband first began to turn on me, to show me who he truly was, I couldn't believe it. For months, I made excuses for his behaviour and deceived myself into thinking he would change and once again become the man I thought I'd married. I don't know if it was my own pride, not wishing to admit that my judgement had been flawed, or a more altruistic inability to believe something so dreadful of someone I loved. Perhaps it was a combination of the two."

"I wonder," she continued, "if Edith suspected that something was wrong, but convinced herself that leaving the village would solve the problem. Or maybe she truly forced herself to believe, out of an inability to even bear to consider alternatives."

"The human mind can be a ghastly thing," Holmes observed. The Woman nodded in agreement.

"Good night, pointy detective," she said then, rising and going to her room. Holmes didn't go to bed that night. He'd never understood how other people could simply turn off their brains in the midst of deep thought, suspending their reasoning processes for hours while their bodies slept. Ever since he could remember, his way had been to think until his brain could think no more, to let the engine run itself out.

He was glad of Watson's presence, but he realised with some measure of surprise that his moments with The Woman were not now as unlike his moments with the doctor as they once had been. Like his flatmate, she had become a friend and then an ally, a trusted listening ear and occasionally, a very useful associate. Her ways were different, but that did not make them unhelpful. He had missed Watson, but he had not been alone, and the realisation made him feel strangely comforted.

A little later a rakish young workman, with a goatee beard and a swagger, lit his clay pipe at the lamp before descending into the street.

—The Adventure of Charles Augustus Milverton

Chapter 11: Irene

When I awoke the following morning, I was filled with what I can only describe as a devilish sense of amusement. I loved having both Holmes and Watson in my house, endlessly amused by their affectionately barbed exchanges. Adding in Mrs Turner and her ways made for a ceaseless buffet of delights for me to savour.

I rose early to see to my bees, who also seemed to be in a buoyant state, though I suppose the impression was in my mind alone. Returning to the house, I found Holmes alone at the table, drinking coffee and going over his notebook. "I've told Watson that he must attempt to infiltrate the Oakhill Farm household today," he said without looking up.

"How will he manage it?" I asked.

"I will be with him," said Holmes, "but in a guise other than my own."

"I see," I answered. "What do you wish me to do?"

"Tell Edith the truth about her husband. Involve Dr Clarke if you must. We may need her help to catch the murderer, and I want to ensure her full cooperation before that happens."

"I think, perhaps, the easiest way would be to produce Julia Rayburn," I said. I wished I hadn't, even though it was true.

"I agree," said Holmes, "but I did not think you would be open to the idea of attempting it."

"I believe it to be the only way of doing what you ask successfully," I answered, feeling my joyful frame of mind evaporate as my thoughts grew darker.

Watson emerged then, looking as fresh as a gentleman on a country holiday. "I hope this is appropriate attire for the day, Holmes," he said, standing at attention in the middle of the floor, as if he were undergoing a military inspection.

"Haven't you brought anything shabbier?" Holmes asked critically.

"No," said the doctor. "I didn't come down with the object of insinuating myself into a farmhouse."

"Very well," groused Holmes.

"I—might have something that would be useful," said the voice of my housekeeper from her vantage point in the kitchen doorway. "I'm afraid it's below Dr Watson's dignity, but I have some clothing that's meant to be donated to the church."

"Excellent," said Holmes. "Bring the possibilities here, please."

A surreal scene followed, in which Mrs Turner surrounded my friend with piles of dingy garments, as if he were a bird in a nest, while Watson and I looked on in amused amazement.

Holmes picked out an outfit worthy of a gardener or farm labourer, a grey shirt and brown trousers that looked as if they had seen much better days. "Here, Watson," he said, "this is far more like it."

The doctor took the clothing gingerly. "Well," he mumbled, "I suppose it's not the worst thing you've ever asked me to do." Mrs Turner looked conflicted, pleased to have been helpful on the one hand, horrified at the impeachment of the doctor's dignity on the other.

"Thank you, Mrs Turner," I said quickly. "You've saved us."

"Yes, indeed," said Dr Watson, blushing. "We'd have been hopeless without you." He turned tail and disappeared to dress himself in the guise Holmes had dictated. The detective vanished as well, to turn himself into whomever he planned to be for the day. I stole a look at my housekeeper, who was still standing motionless in the kitchen doorway with a slight smile on her face.

I waited on the sofa, amused that for once, I was free to remain in my own character while the two men changed theirs. I knew Holmes's love of the drama of disguise, and I was glad that he had a reason to employ it. He would never have admitted it, but it seemed to provide an outlet for the part of him that might have enjoyed treading the boards of the London stage.

Dr Watson emerged quickly, looking more ordinary than I had ever seen him. Normally, there is a pervasive neatness about the doctor, an air that marks him out as a former military man, but Holmes had chosen his clothing well, and he looked like a farmer or one of the working men of the village.

Holmes took longer, but when he came into the sitting room, he looked as ordinary as his friend, an accomplishment that was far more difficult to achieve. I had seen his powers of transformation during the Florida case, but years had elapsed, and I saw with fresh eyes. He smiled at my obvious astonishment.

"I hadn't expected to create such an impression in one accustomed to my methods," he said, clearly pleased with himself.

"You both look your parts very well," I said, not willing to allow him a victory. "I wish you the greatest of luck."

"No need for luck," said Holmes. "Watson and I are old hands at this sort of thing."

"Though I am not usually in disguise," said Watson, not sounding overly pleased at his lot.

"I would hardly call it a disguise, Watson," said his flatmate. "It's merely a way to gain you an entrance. You've no need to speak or act differently than you normally do."

"Well, that's merciful," said the doctor, and I thought I detected a note of sarcasm in his voice.

"Your task, I fear, may be more difficult than ours," said Holmes quietly, looking at me with a steady gaze.

"Difficult but not impossible," I answered. "It will be better, I believe, for Edith to know the truth as quickly as possible."

"Better, perhaps, but no less painful," said my friend, and I was reminded that he understood human emotion far more completely than his reputation indicated.

————

We parted after breakfast, the two men beginning the journey to the farm on foot, which befit the station they planned to imitate. I began my much briefer walk back to the Stevenson house, a journey that felt shorter than I wished it to be, so much did I loathe making it. Ever since Holmes had connected the threads of Julia's shame and Edith's sad deception, I had known that a moment like this must come. If Edith believed in her husband's innocence against the evidence of his own odd behaviour, then it was unlikely, I knew, that she would take the word of someone else without the proof of her own eyes. Whether she would believe that Julia's baby was actually her husband's, I didn't know. I hoped, however, that all of the circumstances would align in such a way that she would be forced to accept the truth, even if she could not do so at first.

My own experience with my late husband's duplicity had taught me the value of the brutal truth. Lies may feel safer and more comfortable, but they are poison. Better to know the ugly reality than a beautiful fiction.

I found Julia pruning flowers in front of her family's home. She smiled when she saw me approach, but her pale face and dark-rimmed eyes showed that she had slept little, if at all. "Good morning, Miss Adler," she said softly, rising and taking my hand.

"Good morning, Julia," I said. "May I have a cup of tea?" I couldn't face broaching the day's subject in the front garden of the Stevenson home. The girl led me to the kitchen, which was part of the servants' domain. I was surprised, but the maids and footmen we passed only nodded, and a few greeted "Miss Julia" as if they were used to her ways.

"Mrs Teague," said Julia, once we reached the environs of the kitchen, "I would like to make Miss Adler a cup of tea." The cook nodded, and I watched as Julia made tea, an act that would have been quite normal for most of the people of the village, but which was, for the daughter of Charles Stevenson, almost an act of rebellion.

Once the tea was made, Julia and I took our places at the servants' table. "Please forgive my eccentricity," said the girl, taking a sip of tea from her china cup. "I've always liked this part of the house best. When I was a little girl, I would come down here and learn all sorts of things from Teague and the others. I can polish a pair of my father's shoes better than either of the current footmen. My parents thought I would grow out of my below-stairs enthrallment, but I never did. My visits became more discreet, but I was still a frequent guest up to the day of my wedding." She flinched after she spoke the last word.

"Don't they mind the fact that you don't keep your place?" I asked, more out of a desire to understand Julia than because I actually wondered. My experience with household servants made me well assured that they were likely to mind a great deal, though they would take pains to appear as if they did not.

"My parents don't know, and the others are used to me. They have to warn any new arrivals, but everyone adjusts in time. I've often thought the staff was more like my family than my parents are," Julia finished. I couldn't help doubting that the hardworking maids and footmen I saw could possibly feel the same way about the privileged daughter of the house.

After a few moments of drinking my tea and bolstering my courage, I began. "Julia, I need you to do something that will be very difficult."

"Anything," she said. "It doesn't matter now." I looked around to confirm that we were fully alone.

"I fear you will feel differently in a moment," I said, speaking quietly. "The truth is, James Phillimore deceived his wife as much as he did you. Rather than disappearing, he left the village on purpose to escape what he claimed was blackmail by Dr Clarke over something that concerned his parents. Edith chose to believe him. We need her help now, but I don't believe we'll be able to get it without you to corroborate your story. It may—it probably will be very difficult, but I see no other way to make Edith comprehend the depth of her husband's deceitfulness."

"Penance is never easy," said Julia.

"It's obvious that Phillimore actually fled to escape his wife finding out about the child and his relationship with you. I assume he convinced you to keep quiet to preserve your own reputation."

"Yes," she answered. "He made it seem like my idea, but he assured me that if I breathed a word of what he'd done, we would go down together. He was afraid, though. I could see it in his eyes the last time we spoke."

"I'm sure, then, that part of his desperation was fear that you would tell his secret."

"He said he had always admired my discretion, and he made it seem like I would be a disappointment to him and to myself if I gave in and told anyone."

"Miss Adler—" she met my eyes with fire in her own. "I'm glad Ed knows. Please, when I'm gone, tell him that I helped you. He might not think so ill of me if he knew."

"Tell him yourself," I said, feeling a flash of something that was either inspiration or madness. "Speak to him before you go. You must agree that you at least owe him that."

"You're sure he'll see me?" she asked.

"I'm sure," I said.

"Very well," she answered, her eyes fixed on her pale hand as it rested on the table. "If you believe he wishes it, I will do so."

"I'm convinced he wishes it more than you can bear to believe," I answered.

———

Julia and I drove to the farm in silence. I had nothing more to tell her, since her part in the day's events would depend on Edith as much as on either of us. I simply hoped I could avoid causing a scene that would bring unbearable pain to either of the two women. I like to pride myself on a certain measure of emotional objectivity, but I could not manage to detach myself from my dread of what I was about to undertake.

We gained admittance to the house easily, and we were shown into the parlour, where Edith soon joined us. She looked surprised when she saw Julia, but I saw something flash across her face as she came into the room that suggested she might not be as shocked at what we were there to reveal as I'd feared.

"Now, Watson, the fair sex is your department," said Holmes, with a smile, when the dwindling frou-frou of skirts had ended in the slam of the front door.

—The Adventure of the Second Stain

Chapter 12: Holmes

The detective and the doctor reached the Phillimore farm by midmorning, but instead of going to the house, they made their way across the fields to the gathering of homes where the workers lived with their wives. "I thought we were to infiltrate the household," said Watson, who looked confused, but followed his flatmate in the usual way.

"So we are, in a manner of speaking," said Holmes, "but I happen to know that the cook is married to one of the men, and today is her day off. We will find her in her lair."

Watson sighed wearily, and Holmes stopped and looked at him for a moment. "I'm sorry, old friend. I didn't mean to sap your strength."

"No matter," said Watson. "It's only my old injury. Perhaps if you tell me more about what I'm to do, it will help distract my mind from the discomfort."

"Very well," said Holmes. "We know that Mrs Merriwether acted as an emissary of sorts between Phillimore and his wife, meaning that she was aware of Phillimore's whereabouts. According to Eliza, the murdered man's young daughter, Mrs Merriwether was also the first person called by Edith Phillimore when the child found the body."

"The child found the body? How dreadful for her," Watson interjected with a pained expression on his amiable face.

"She seemed to handle it decently enough," said Holmes. "She thought her father was asleep."

"Seeming is different from being," said the doctor. "I have attended at the homes of many children who were the unfortunate discoverers of a parent's death, and not one of them was without a scar of some sort."

"Set your mind at ease," said Holmes. "I spoke to her afterward and explained the truth."

"Very well," said Watson. "Having witnessed your uncanny way with the children of London, I can hardly fail to believe in your capability when it comes to a child of Fulworth."

"Your concern does you credit," said Holmes.

"Our story," the detective continued, "is that we are looking for work and heard that Mr Merriwether might be hiring extra hands. He's in charge of the labourers and takes responsibility for many of those things. Of course, Oakhill Farm isn't looking to take anyone on, and we won't find Merriwether at home. Once we gain admittance, however, you can begin to work your usual magic on the cook."

"Why not go alone?" Watson asked. "You know the case much better than I do, and you're familiar with the lady in question."

"Unfortunately," said Holmes, "familiarity is not a blessing in the present circumstance. She deplores me in my normal guise. I believe I will succeed in not being recognised if I act like your nearly-mute friend. If I went alone, however, the risk of discovery would be much greater. Besides, Watson, you are far too modest. I have nowhere near your ability to put ladies of all ages and societal stations at their ease, nor do I wish to cultivate it."

"Your confidence in me is touching," answered Watson drily. "If I am unable to succeed in gaining the information you require, what will you do then?"

"I have every assurance that your conversation will be beneficial, but I will explore other avenues to the same conclusion if I must," said Holmes.

"I left my revolver at the cottage," said Watson.

"No matter," his friend replied mildly. "I picked it up myself. Normally I would not take it upon myself to carry your weapon, but in the present situation, I will take your place as the silent witness with his hand on the trigger."

"You mock me, Holmes," said the doctor. "It's not sporting."

"Certainly not," rejoined the detective. "Your silent vigilance has saved us from a tight spot many a time, and I'm not likely to forget it."

Finally, the two men reached a row of modest homes. Outside of the first, they found a girl putting clothes on a line. Her dress was torn, and she looked tired, but she smiled in a friendly way. "Where might we find the home of Mr Merriwether?" Watson asked, returning her smile.

"It's just there," she said, pointing to a house three down from her own. It was a drab grey colour, much weathered by wind and rain, but respectably kept and slightly larger than the others around it. Holmes noticed that the girl did not look entirely pleased at the question, and as they turned to move on, she called after them, "You won't get any help there."

"I fear she's correct," said Watson, once the two were out of earshot and nearly to the Merriwether home.

"You are determined to sell yourself short," said Holmes. "Besides, I'll be here to rescue you if anything goes wildly amiss." His flatmate shook his head resignedly and followed the detective up to the door.

As Holmes had predicted, it was opened by the cook. Instead of her usual white apron over a practical grey frock, she was dressed in a garish yellow colour that reminded Holmes of the time he'd seen a child get ill on a train from London to Birmingham.

"What do you want?" she asked suspiciously.

"Please excuse our intrusion," Watson answered smoothly. "My friend and I are looking for work and thought your husband might have some to offer."

Mrs Merriwether looked the doctor up and down. "Well," she said, "you don't talk like most of the men around here, and I rarely have visitors. Come inside and have a cup of tea."

"Thank you," said Watson. "That would be very welcome." The two men followed the cook into a small parlour that was as drab as the outside of the house, but neat. Holmes scrunched himself into the corner of a threadbare chair, folding into himself so that he would look like the more insignificant of the two companions, while Watson took his place on the doily-covered sofa. The lady of the house went to fetch something edible, and Holmes tried to look as if he didn't notice the irritated look Watson bestowed upon him.

When Mrs Merriwether returned, she bore a plate of iced biscuits that instantly repulsed the detective. He took one, however, along with a cup of tea that appeared more promising. "Now," said the lady when both men had been served, "what sort of work were you looking for?" She fixed Watson with a sharply appraising stare. "You don't seem much like a field worker, not with those hands."

Well done, thought Holmes, willing to acknowledge merit wherever he happened to find it. The doctor looked momentarily discomfited, but he rallied quickly. "My name is John Morstan. I'm a veterinary surgeon, and this is my friend Smith who assists me with the larger stock. I thought some of the animals might need looking after. I understand your husband has oversight of them."

"No," she said, "for that you'd need Peter Warren, but Williams was just by not a week ago, and he looked them all over. Won't be needing any more of your kind."

"That is unfortunate," said the doctor. "I haven't had biscuits as good as these since my wife passed away. It's a pity we'll have to move on without tasting more." The cook blushed with pleasure at the compliment.

Watson had a gift. Holmes couldn't deny it. He might not be brilliant, but he was certainly skilled. The combination of compliment and pitiable revelation had obviously begun to win the woman over.

"Stay and have a few more, then," she said. "It's not often I get to entertain in my own home. They're always running me ragged at the big house."

"That must be difficult," said Watson, "especially given the excitement of the past few days."

"Heard about that, have you?" she asked. "I suppose it's all over the county now."

"I'm sure it must have been terrible for you," said the doctor, "losing a member of the family with whom you have such a close association."

The cook sniffed meaningfully. "I don't mean," she said. "Never could bear the man. I only stayed around because of his wife, Edith Pope, as was. For her sake, I never said it when he was alive, but it doesn't seem to matter now."

"Oh," said Watson, "I understood him to have been a very pleasant man." Holmes had told him nothing of the sort.

"People always say the most ridiculous things about the dead," said the woman. "He was a bad-tempered man until the day he disappeared. His only redeeming quality was his love for Edith, but even that failed at the end."

"I see," said the doctor. "How did it fail?" He had gone too far. Holmes could feel the woman's reticence return in an instant.

"Nothing worth speaking about," she said. "I ought to get back to my mending. I'm sorry I couldn't be of more help." She ushered the two men out the door as if she was afraid to keep them in her house.

Once outside, Watson shook his head dejectedly. "I told you it would come to nothing," he said. "I'm not cut out for this sort of thing."

"Not at all," said Holmes pleasantly. "You did brilliantly."

"What do you mean?" asked his flatmate. "She barely spoke before I ruined the whole thing."

"My dear Watson," said Holmes, "you must learn to view these things with a more careful eye. It is true that Mrs Merriwether did not reveal the entire plan of Phillimore's flight and her involvement in it, but I hardly expected her to do so, and I know some of her part anyway. What she did reveal is that she was aware, at least to some extent, of James Phillimore's marital indiscretions. Her inclusion of the phrase 'at the end' suggests strongly that she was speaking of his relationship with Julia Rayburn."

Watson stared at his friend, and Holmes let out a dry laugh. "Well," said the doctor, "if I've been of help, then I'm pleased."

"Always, my friend," said Holmes, leading him back across the fields.

———

The two men returned to the cottage, and Holmes transformed himself back into his usual guise. He could feel his brain working to make cohesive sense of the fractured pieces of information he now possessed, so he took his black notebook in hand and went to Irene's bees.

The detective spent the next half hour simply observing. First, he watched every tiny movement as if it were its own single event. Only after he had done that did he allow himself to watch them all together, to see the elaborate dance that made up the life of the hive. Such was the case, he thought. Such was every case, every collection of seemingly disparate events that nonetheless affected each other and connected intrinsically with one another.

A man was dead. That was the beginning point, no matter where it fell in the narrative. The man had left home to escape the consequences of an illicit affair, ostensibly to never return. Instead, he had been killed and his body dumped in a prominent location at his own farm. Supposedly, only two people had known of the affair, the two who had engaged in it. But there was a third. The cook had known something, and that meant that others might know as well. The important question was who and what they had chosen to do with the information. That, Holmes realised, was almost certainly the key to unravelling the whole mystery of Phillimore's death.

In an experience of women which extends over many nations and three separate continents, I have never looked upon a face which gave a clearer promise of a refined and sensitive nature.

—The Sign of Four

Chapter 13: Irene

"Inspector Graves just left," said Edith as she took a seat across from Julia and me. "They've been combing the grounds again, looking for new evidence, but they can't find anything."

"I'm sorry," I said. "That must be very difficult for you."

"I would put up with a lot more if it would help them find my husband's murderer," she said, and I took my opportunity, fearing that if I did not do so right away, I wouldn't manage it at all.

"That's why we've come," I said. "We want to tell you something that may have power to alter your view of events. I'm afraid—" I looked over at Julia, who was deathly pale, "that it may also prove distressing for you, and for that I apologise in advance."

Edith laughed. "I hardly see what could be more distressing than what I've already experienced."

Suddenly, I wanted to laugh, in that horrible, untimely way that hits one at funerals or at the most sombre moments in church. The irony was piercing. I stifled the laugh, but as a result, there was a moment of quiet.

"Miss Adler, I'll do it myself," said Julia very softly, finally breaking the heavy silence.

I looked at her in surprise. "Would you like to be alone?"

"Yes," she answered, with her old resolve back in her voice. Edith's expression was guarded, and I had no idea what she might be thinking or anticipating, but I trusted Julia, so I took my leave and went outside. Truthfully, I was delighted to be relieved of an unpleasant task, and it seemed like a certain kind of poetic justice for Julia to be the bearer of the news.

The midmorning was slightly cool, and I took the path away from the house, not really intending to do anything in particular but hoping I might observe something useful. I had spent so much time at the farm over the previous few days that it seemed impossible that I would miss anything that hadn't been there before.

As I approached the barn, I saw two men standing outside the door, and I heard one of them say, "I don't understand why we're even working. Phillimore's dead, and his wife don't care one way or the other."

"We will work as long as there's work to be done," answered another voice, and Peter Warren appeared at the door to the barn. He saw me and removed his cap, which caused the other two to turn and do the same.

"Forgive me," I said. "I had no intention of disturbing your work."

"Seems to me, Miss Adler," said the tall foreman, "that you're very good at disturbing people's work." I was prepared to be affronted, but he smiled then, and his smile changed his face so completely that I was amazed. No longer was he the severe man I'd imagined him to be; instead, he was the husband and father I'd never quite been able to picture him being.

He came toward me and spoke quietly. "The little girl's in the carriage house. She might need some company."

"Thank you," I answered. I didn't wish to walk through the barn and endure more stares, so I went back around to the outside entrance, thinking as I did so that James Phillimore would never again drive out of it, except if he were to do so in his ghostly form. It was an extremely fanciful image, but I could almost visualise the spectre of the dead man riding restlessly through the grounds of his farm.

I dismissed the picture from my mind as I crept back to the dark corner where Eliza had brought me before. The sound that greeted me was one I hadn't heard before; she was crying.

As quickly as I could, I sat down on the dirty floor and gathered her close, rocking her in my arms. She clung to me and buried her wet face in my shoulder, holding Charles tightly. "They took all my things away," she sobbed, her voice muffled by the cloth of my green shirtwaist.

"I'm so sorry, darling," I said. "It was dreadful of them. We must bring new things."

"No!" she said, shaking her head emphatically against me. I just held her then, not knowing what to say to ease her sadness. I am no psychologist, but I wondered how many of her tears were due to the death of her father and how many to the maelstrom around her.

After a long time, she sat up and wiped her eyes with the back of her hand. "Is Mr Holmes here?"

"Not now," I said, smiling.

"Charles wanted to see him," she said.

"Then he shall," I answered. "You and he and Mummy must come to my house very soon." This seemed to content her. She leaned against me once again, and very soon, she fell asleep.

I carried Eliza, who was heavier than she looked, back to the servants' entrance of the house and handed her to Lewis the maid, who smiled at the sight of her sleeping form. I didn't relish the thought of returning to the cold parlour where the two women were, but didn't think I could forestall it any longer. With head held high, I made my way back to the front of the house, determined to make the best of whatever sight was to greet me.

I don't know what I expected, but I certainly did not anticipate finding Edith Phillimore holding Julia Rayburn's hand gently and smiling at her with a look of genuine peace that I hadn't seen on her face for some time.

Both women looked up when I entered. "Sorry to intrude," I said, feeling like I'd been apologising a great deal that day, something that is not my usual practise.

"It's all right," said Julia, and I saw traces of tears on her face, though she smiled at me.

"I understand," said Edith, "and I will help any way I can, though Julia and I both ask, if possible, that my husband's—associations be kept private, if they may be."

"I will do the very best I can," I said, "and Mr Holmes has no intention of publicising them."

"I know that it may not be possible," said Julia, "but for my husband's sake, I hope that it is." I wondered to myself what Edith might have said to her on that topic, but I didn't pry, and our ride back to the village was as silent as our ride to the farm had been until we were nearly to the Stevenson house.

"Thank you for that," said Julia suddenly.

"You have yourself to thank," I said. "I was just the messenger."

She laughed. "That's what you really think, isn't it? No wonder you and Mr Holmes get on so well."

I left her at her parents' home, but extracted a promise from her that she wouldn't leave Fulworth until the conclusion of the case, which she was only willing to give on the assurance that she might be needed by Edith, depending on developments.

I made my way back up the hill, glad that I did not know what had passed between the two women. Edith had surprised me slightly, though I thought I understood her reaction. There's a kind of stubbornness that clings to a flawed way of thinking but is actually relieved to be proven wrong, to have legitimate doubts confirmed. I had known that stubbornness and the relief that comes from being delivered of it.

———

When I reached home, I went to check on my bees and found that they had a strange companion, a detective with long fingers and luminous eyes. "Hello, Irene," he said without turning around as I came up behind him.

"Hullo, Holmes."

"The bees seem well contented," he mused.

"They are," I answered. "I am happy to say that their care is rather less complicated than solving criminal cases."

"I don't know," said my friend. "Both are a matter of small parts that fit into a unified whole."

"When it comes to the murder of James Phillimore, I fear that I understand a great deal of the parts and very little of the whole," I admitted.

"Well, Watson and I were not entirely unsuccessful," said Holmes. "Come inside, and we shall tell you our discovery."

"Poor Watson," I said.

"Not so," said Holmes. "He performed his task with success."

———

When my friend and I reached the cottage, we found Dr Watson and Mrs Turner conversing congenially over cold meat pies. The sight of food reminded my stomach that it was starving, and I sat down to relieve my hunger pangs. Holmes didn't seem to notice the spread, making his way to the wing chair instead. My curiosity warred with my hunger, but physical cravings won out over mental ones, and I began to eat.

"I hope your errand was successful," said the doctor kindly.

"Very," I answered between mouthfuls. "Edith Phillimore is fully on our side and apprised of the situation."

"I can't help feeling our task was less elegantly done," said Watson, "but Holmes seems to have gleaned something useful out of it."

I noticed that Mrs Turner smiled a great deal whenever the shorter man spoke, though she did not comment. It was her usual habit to eat her meals with me, but I had been surprised at her readiness to do so with my guests, not from any reticence on my part but an expected hesitation on hers. I was beginning, I thought, to understand.

I ate quickly, wanting to combine my thoughts with Holmes's as quickly as I could, wondering if he had come any closer to apprehending what was still impenetrable to me. When I'd had my fill, I rose from the table. "Excuse me," I said to doctor and housekeeper, "please don't feel the need to hurry. I wish to discuss the morning with Holmes."

Dr Watson nodded. "Yes, before you came, Mrs Turner was telling me about some of the local legends. I would like to hear more if she isn't bored with the subject." The lady in question blushed like a schoolgirl and showed no sign of leaving the table.

I joined my friend in the other room, surprised to realise how comfortable I felt as I settled onto the sofa and looked at his face with its languid expression that denoted acute mental activity. "Now, Holmes," I said, "relieve my misery and tell me the result of your attempt at Mrs Merriwether."

"Watson's attempt," he corrected. "I'm happy to say that our mutual friend more than outdid himself, albeit somewhat accidentally."

"I'm well aware of Dr Watson's talents," I said sharply, not meaning the comment ironically, though given what was occurring at my table at that moment, I suppose it was.

"Very well," said Holmes, with infuriating mildness. "We went to the woman's house, were treated as strangers, and Watson engaged her on the subject of the Phillimore murder after a well-placed comment on the excellence of her iced biscuits."

I laughed. "I take it she said something significant."

"She spoke few words, but she insinuated that she knew Phillimore had not been faithful to his wife. More specific she would not be, but she certainly knew something."

"If she knew, why would she not have told Edith?"

"It's a fascinating question to ponder," said Holmes. "Given her vital role in the man's flight, I expect that she intended to tell Edith at a later date and convince her to never rejoin her husband once he had left. She seems uncommonly attached to her."

"That I can corroborate," I said, "but mightn't she be the murderer?"

"A sour disposition does not necessarily single one out as a killer," said Holmes, smiling. "A murderer would have been far more careful with his words than she was, though I believe our appearing to be strangers loosened her lips to an unusual extent. At any rate, I don't believe she killed the man."

"I suppose it's helpful to rule her out as a suspect," I said.

"Very," said Holmes, "but the question now is, would she have told someone, and if so, who?"

"I fear we have a great many possibilities," I said.

"Fewer, perhaps, than it seems at first blush," said my friend, his voice taking on a schoolmasterly tone. "In every case, there is a limited number of concerned individuals with probable involvement. If none of them prove to be the culprit, then the gaze must widen, but the first task must be to rule each of them out."

"We know that neither Edith nor Julia was aware that she knew. We can also rule out Phillimore himself because he must have known she was to be in charge of the posting of the rabbit, and he would have been very unlikely to trust her or quietly allow his wife to do so if he'd known. Warren, one of the police's favourites, is clearly unaware, or he would have used the information to throw suspicion off himself. Dr Clarke, who by rights shouldn't even be involved, would certainly have told me if he'd suspected anything. We know Julia didn't consult him or the midwife, so that's another pathway taken to its conclusion."

"Julia's father," I said. "We don't know why Charles Stevenson was there." Suddenly, a host of possibilities crowded into my mind that hadn't been there before I'd learned Julia's secret. Her revelation and the subsequent events had banished her father's presence from my mind, but the memory of my encounter with him in the Phillimore parlour rushed back forcefully.

"Precisely," said Holmes, and I could see with infuriating clarity that he had known where the conversation was headed all along and was simply waiting for me to catch up to his reasoning.

"Clearly, you're ahead of me," I said, a trifle testily. "What do you have in mind?"

"I plan to visit him this afternoon. Do you care to join me?"

"I hadn't anticipated such a direct approach," I answered.

"Give me a small amount of credit," said Holmes. "I don't plan to greet the man with an accusation of guilt. I have my methods of encouraging revelation."

"Very well," I answered, "but don't expect an easy time of it. He's unpleasant at the best of times."

"Watson," called Holmes to his flatmate, who was still at the table conversing animatedly with my housekeeper, "three will be too many for this task, I fear. If you are favourably disposed, Miss Adler and I will leave you to your own devices."

"Certainly," said the doctor, looking excessively pleased.

———

"Holmes, you are positively a romantic," I said as we strolled down the lane that would take us to the office of Charles Stevenson.

"Nothing of the sort," he retorted.

"You can't claim," I replied, "that you are ignorant of the attachment currently developing within the walls of my house."

"Watson," said the detective, "has many talents, one of which is the ability to form absurdly rash attachments."

"But is it rash?" I asked. "He has known Mrs Turner for some time, and she has always admired him."

I looked up at my friend with a mischievous glint in my eye. "Holmes, I believe you would consider attachment of any kind to be unforgivably rash, except that of yourself to your chemistry set."

"Nonsense, Irene," he answered. "I'm at least as attached to my tobacco." My laugh rang out in the clear, open air.

Presently, I spoke again. "If there is a perfectly logical explanation for Stevenson's presence at the farm, what do you intend to do?"

"If that happens," he said, "we will follow the clues and see where else they lead us. I do not believe, however, that we will have to concern ourselves with that."

"You believe Stevenson is the murderer?"

My friend spoke soberly. "I deal in certainties rather than probabilities, but I saw something interesting as Watson and I made our way back to the village. Another person was making his way toward the farm workers' cottages. He was far away, but I could tell by his gait and shape that it was the man I had seen standing over Phillimore's body."

"Stevenson was going to speak to Mrs Merriwether?"

"I am not certain," he answered, "but it's highly suggestive. None of the families who live in those houses could ever hope to afford his services, so it's unlikely he would have been calling in his professional capacity. It's also hard to imagine a man with his love of outdoing his neighbours idly visiting one of the poorest places in the area unless he had a pressing reason."

"Upon my word, Holmes," I said, "will you never stop concealing vital clues from me?"

"I meant no such thing," he answered calmly. "I merely meant to give your mind ample time to process our earlier conversation before I added this development." I folded my arms, irritated.

"That hurts my pride, Watson," he said at last. "It is a petty feeling, no doubt, but it hurts my pride."

—The Five Orange Pips

Chapter 14: Holmes

The detective continued, undaunted by his companion's annoyance. "I also wished to share the information right before we see the man. I thought it might inflame you to your present state of aggravation, which I hope will prove helpful in our exchange."

In a moment, The Woman had stepped in front of Holmes and turned around, effectively barring him from continuing down the lane. He looked down at her with a mixture of amusement and perplexity.

"I am glad I'm able to provide you with the day's entertainment," she said, "but before we continue to the man's house, I insist on a full explanation of what you intend to do. I have been content with limited information when my own safety was in question, but I see no reason such reticence should be necessary now."

"No matter," said Holmes. "It's just that I had anticipated the value of having someone with me who is less knowledgeable and therefore likely to perform naturally."

Irene sniffed. "Holmes, your powers of manipulation grow ever larger with each passing day. Dr Watson credits you with a straightforwardness that you begin to lack. Perhaps I should tell the poor man to watch out for your machinations." She spit out the words with great pique, but as she did so, she moved out of the way and allowed the detective to continue walking.

"I take it you agree to leave me to my methods," said the detective mildly.

"I wish I didn't trust you as much as I do," said The Woman. "I will consent to be the ignorant partner. Do you have anything you wish me to say or do?" As much as she tried to seem resigned, she was, he thought, also filled with a conspiratorial sense of excitement.

"Simply play along and act as you normally would," said Holmes.

"Very well," she answered, as they approached the low brick building that housed the office of Charles Stevenson.

A ring of the bell produced a short young man who looked as if he was so clean he was likely to sweat soapsuds if warmed. "What is your business?" he asked curtly. "You have no appointment."

Holmes cleared his throat. "Please inform Mr Stevenson that Sherlock Holmes and Irene Adler wish to speak with him."

The young man looked up at the detective, seeming to evaluate whether or not it was within his ability to get rid of the visitors himself. Holmes stared down at him sharply until he dropped his gaze and ushered the companions inside, disappearing behind a closed door.

The barrister's vestibule was furnished simply, but the wood of the young clerk's desk was of the highest quality, as was the bench on which Holmes and Irene took their seats without being asked. The companions waited five minutes and then ten. "Do you think he means to bore us into losing interest?" asked The Woman.

"No," said the detective, "but he does mean to make us uncomfortable, something he does very well in the courtroom, I'd imagine."

"Have you never seen him perform his role as legal advocate?" Irene enquired. "I understood him to be very active in London."

"I have heard of him, but our paths have not crossed," said Holmes. "I would expect him to have heard of me."

The door opened again, and out stepped Charles Stevenson, barrister, wearing a suit that Holmes priced at roughly the yearly income of one of the men who worked on the Phillimore farm. "Please come in," said his smooth voice, and the detective and his companion passed into a large, dark office. The clerk went back to his desk, giving Holmes a cold glance as he did so.

"You'll have to forgive my young man," said Stevenson, motioning to the two to sit down. "His father is a peer, and it seems to have affected his disposition." He laughed drily. "A peer with no money to speak of, but still, a peer." Holmes thought that it must have been one of the man's great regrets that he himself had not been born to rank.

Stevenson sat down behind his desk and folded his long, pale fingers. "Well, Mr Holmes," he said, "I can't fathom that the great detective of Baker Street has come to me for legal advocacy."

"I would like your help," said Holmes deferentially. "I've been retained by Edith Phillimore to investigate the circumstances of her husband's unfortunate death, but I find the details very difficult to unravel," he lied smoothly. "If you have any information that might help, I'd be indebted to you. As you know, villages are very difficult places to glean anything of value. A great deal of talk goes on, without clarity or intelligence."

The barrister smiled. "I hardly think that you, Mr Holmes, would be foiled by the unreliability of village gossip. I thank you for your flattery, but it is unnecessary. I will help you in any way I can."

Holmes smiled. "Excellent. As you were on hand the day the body was discovered, I hoped you might shed a little light on the circumstances. I've spoken to Dr Clarke, but he was so focused on the corpse that I fear he may have missed some of the surrounding details that a man of your expertise would have noticed."

Stevenson leaned forward, and his fine white hair fell over his forehead. The detective noted that he appeared to relish the opportunity to give his account. "I only learned of the unfortunate event because I was supping at the home of the good doctor that night. We went to the house together and found them laying out the poor man's body. It was obvious he'd been killed long before, but still an arresting sight. The widow was distraught."

"If you don't mind a question, who fetched the doctor?"

"Mrs Merriwether, the cook at Oakhill Farm."

"Were the police present when you arrived?"

"Only just. Graves has been resident in the village for the duration of the investigation of the disappearance, and he roused Chipping and those ridiculous boys. It's a good thing they didn't find any evidence. With their methods, I doubt it would hold up in court."

"You favour the London police, then?" asked Holmes.

"On the contrary," said Stevenson. "They're equally inept, but with fancier pedigrees." Holmes didn't particularly like the man, but he had to agree. "I remained at the house until Dr Clarke left. Miss Adler saw me just prior to our departure."

"True," said Irene.

"Had you any theories about Phillimore's disappearance before that time?" Holmes asked.

"None whatsoever," said Stevenson.

"Thank you," said Holmes, "you've been very helpful," though he was thinking the opposite. "Miss Adler, I believe we may take our leave."

"Won't you stay for a cup of tea?" asked the barrister, looking as if he didn't mean it.

"I think not," said Holmes. "We have other pressing engagements." The young man showed the detective and The Woman out in the manner of a housewife throwing rubbish into the dustbin.

Once outside, Irene looked up at Holmes in perplexity. "If you've managed to glean something important from that conversation, then you've outstripped me by miles."

"Few miles," Holmes answered. "The man is less susceptible to appeals to his vanity than I'd anticipated. We do know now that Mrs Merriwether sounded the initial alarm, though this was a frustratingly elaborate way to arrive at that detail."

"I don't believe my ignorance was of much assistance after all," said Irene, "though I did appreciate your subservient act."

"I confess," said Holmes, "that I hoped the man would betray that he knew something of his daughter's predicament."

"An excellent motive," The Woman murmured.

"Still a possible one," said Holmes, "but if it is true, we will have to discover it by different means."

"I almost think I prefer cases in which my own life is in danger," said Irene. "The excitement is much enhanced."

"Stay the course," said Holmes. "We will find the murderer."

"Do you not worry that he or she will have fled?"

"No," said Holmes. "A person who places a corpse or arranges for a corpse to be placed in as prominent a location as Phillimore's murderer did is almost certain to remain and survey the effects of his handiwork."

"Insanity?"

"Not necessarily, but a desire for recognition, certainly."

"Then why not confess, as some do, and receive all the credit?"

"I believe our murderer feels stronger than that, invincible and not susceptible to detection. Of course, in truth, all murderers are susceptible to detection because they invariably make mistakes."

Holmes would have continued to speak, but as he and Irene turned to start up the hill to the cottage, a yell behind them stopped them in their tracks. The detective turned to see the frantic form of Edith Phillimore, flushed and wild-eyed as she approached.

"Whatever is the matter?" asked Irene.

"It's Eliza," panted the breathless woman. "I can't find her anywhere."

I confess that I have been as blind as a mole, but it is better to learn wisdom late than never to learn it at all.

—The Man with the Twisted Lip

Chapter 15: Irene

"What happened?" I asked, putting out a hand and lightly touching Edith's shoulder. "She was at home earlier. I saw her in the carriage house, and then Lewis put her to bed."

"I know," she answered. "She got up and went to the chicken house, and she never came back. I sent the men scouring all over the property for her, but she was gone. There's no chance she had enough time to get away under her own power."

"Have you told the police?" Holmes asked.

She nodded. "They're forming a search party, but I came straight to you from them." I had observed that while Holmes did not admire the police's methods when it came to more refined tasks, he had the sense to see when they were needed.

"Of course, we will do all we can," said Holmes.

I could see that Edith was near tears, but she used powerful self-control to hold herself together for the moment. "Inspector Graves told me to go home and wait for developments," she said. "I'm going to ask Julia to come with me."

"Very wise," said Holmes, and she walked away toward the Stevenson house, her shoulders bowed with dejection and fear.

"What do we do?" I asked my friend.

"We go home," said Holmes.

"Whatever for?"

"To figure out what I've missed."

———

The inside of the cottage was empty, and it didn't take Holmes to deduce for me that Dr Watson and Mrs Turner had gone out together. My friend immediately made for the wing chair, and I sat opposite him so that he could talk through the details in his mind if he wished. He was beyond me then. I saw facts, and my brain refused to stop making surmises, but I had no idea which direction to proceed or what might be in my companion's mind. After a long silence, I got up to make tea, but when I came back and pushed a cup into Holmes's hand, he did not acknowledge my presence.

"Tobacco," he said after what seemed like an age. I was almost asleep by this point, drowsy amidst the quiet of his thoughts, but the insistent tone of his voice woke me, even though he spoke quietly.

"What?" I asked.

Holmes leapt to his feet, colour rising in his cheeks. "We must leave at once. There is no time to lose." I knew better than to argue, following him outside as quickly as I could.

"The tobacco, Irene. He tried to fool me, but the tobacco gave him away."

"Who, Phillimore? Stevenson?" I breathed hard, trying to keep pace with Holmes's long, quick strides.

"No," he said, "Dr Clarke."

"What?" I said again, walking along and staring at my friend with disbelief. "I thought we ruled out the possibility of Edith's story."

"We did," said Holmes, "but nevertheless, it's him. I saw traces of Phillimore's tobacco in his study."

"How do you know it was Phillimore's and not someone else's who uses the same sort?"

"Clarke doesn't smoke, and he never allowed tobacco anywhere near him from notions of it being harmful to the health. The traces I saw were ground into the floor of his study, as if dropped by accident and not heeded. He would never have allowed the stuff if he could have helped it. The pattern of droppings suggests that the tobacco fell out of Phillimore's pocket, perhaps during an altercation." Holmes related these facts in a monotone that suggested he was agitated on the inside. I wondered why these signs had not been evident to him before, but I didn't comment. There would be plenty of time for that.

I quickly ascertained that Holmes was leading me to Dr Clarke's house at the edge of the village. A shouted greeting by Miss Rose as we passed the butcher's shop was not returned, and I hoped in passing that I had not mortally offended her.

"We won't find Clarke here," said Holmes. "I only hope to find clues to where he might have taken the child."

"Should I find the police?"

"No," said Holmes. "They will be half way to the farm by now. There isn't time."

Clarke's house was dark and quiet, with no sign of anyone to let us in. Holmes dexterously picked the lock on the front door and led me through the suite of rooms that the doctor used as a surgery. The light from the afternoon sun cast strange shadows, and I felt a strong sense of foreboding as I looked around at the coldly formal arrangements. Holmes quickly passed through, entering an unusually broad hallway.

"What are we seeking?" I asked.

"Any sign of the child and where he might have taken her," said Holmes briefly. "Barring that, any sort of disturbance."

My friend undoubtedly knew what he meant by this, but I was less sure. I found myself peeking into obviously-unused rooms and then coming out again into the passage, feeling as if I were Alice in Wonderland trying to make sense of a strange world. Holmes, meanwhile, went straight for a large room at the end. After a few minutes, I joined him, less than satisfied with my own efforts. He was searching Clarke's dustbin.

I knew better than to say anything and proceeded to walk around the perimeter of the room with as little luck as I'd had previously. I was about to give up and search through the jumbled papers on Clarke's vast desk, a task Holmes had already performed, when something caught my eye. There was a flash of white tucked between the cushion and the back of Clarke's chair. It was the smallest of fibres, but it looked out of place.

"Holmes," I said, "look."

To his credit, the detective trusted me enough to stand to his feet and look at the wisps in my hand. "Charles the rabbit," he said shortly. "Eliza was here." As gratifying as the realisation was, it also chilled my blood. Until we had found evidence, the reality of Eliza's kidnapping had seemed further off, almost as if it might not really be happening. Now, there was no mistaking the truth.

I stood back as Holmes made his way around the room again, looking at each surface. Finally, he glanced over to where I was, standing next to a small table on which the doctor had placed a decanter and a glass. The detective ran toward me and grabbed the glass, putting it to his lips and turning it slowly. His eyes grew alarmingly bright.

"They're here!" he said

"What?" I asked dumbly, unable to process what he was saying.

"The lip of the glass is warmer than it should be," he whispered. "Speak softly."

"There's no need for that," said a voice in the doorway, and a woman with a ramrod-straight spine, a black dress, and a large gun met my gaze.

"Mrs Parkfield," I said pointlessly.

"I've no idea what you hope to accomplish," Holmes said coolly. "You can't possibly keep us here."

"I have no intention of keeping you after Dr Clarke gets what he wants." She trained her gun on me. "This is quite simple, Mr Holmes," she said, and the detective and I sat down in the chairs that stood before Clarke's desk. I looked over at Holmes, trying to ascertain what work his brain might be doing, but his face was totally impassive. Mrs Parkfield sat in Clarke's chair, not taking her eyes off either of us. I had never liked her when I'd met her in the village, and my ill feeling was finally justified.

My mind went back to the day I had been held prisoner in a tiny field office in south Florida. I had felt hopeless then, but the circumstances were hardly the same. Holmes had been with me then as well, but I had been unaware of his presence, ignorant of the fact that he was about to rescue me. Now, he was seated next to me, and his presence was comforting, though the irony was that he, too, was a prisoner.

After a few short moments that seemed much longer than they really were, I heard a noise in the hallway, and Clarke passed the doorway with the sleeping Eliza Phillimore in his arms. He stepped into his study, and I saw that the child was more than asleep; she had obviously been drugged.

"What is the meaning of this, Clarke?" asked Holmes, not as if he was addressing a criminal as much as an old and disappointing friend.

"It's your fault, you know," said Clarke. "I was getting away with it before you came. When you arrived and started nosing your way around the village, I knew it was only a matter of time before you figured out the truth one way or the other. After all, you learned some of your methods from me, though you've far eclipsed my modest achievements."

"What do you want from me?" asked Holmes.

"You're going to write to the police, assuring them of the guilt of Charles Stevenson for the death of James Phillimore, a murder motivated by the fact that the man had meddled with Stevenson's daughter Julia. Miss Adler will deliver this letter, along with proof in the form of letters in the man's own hand—or the hand of someone near enough for the ineptitude of Inspector Graves. Mrs Parkfield, my trusted assistant, will make sure this occurs. After that, I will personally escort both of you to the train station. You will leave Fulworth, never to return. After that, and only after that, I will return Eliza to her unfortunate mother. You must see, Holmes, that for all your cleverness, you have no option. I don't want to hurt you."

"Very well," said Holmes, sounding defeated. Mrs Parkfield smiled unpleasantly and handed him a piece of stationery and a pen, her gun still pointed firmly in my direction. The detective went to the side table and placed the paper upon it, beginning to write, his non-dominant hand fidgeting nervously in his pocket. Clarke watched him carefully. "It's dull," he said after a moment of wrestling with the pen.

"Mrs Parkfield, get him another," said Clarke, his old shoulders slumping from the little girl's weight.

At that moment, Holmes's lazily fidgeting hand sprang to life, and I saw a blur of light that suddenly blazed up with heat and shooting sparks. At the same time, the decanter rolled toward me across the floor, and in a split second, Holmes had snatched Eliza from the dazed Clarke, and we ran for the door.

"Fire! Fire!" screamed my companion as we hurled ourselves outside, and one of the inevitabilities of village life began to work immediately in our favour. People came running from everywhere. Mothers streamed out of Cottonwood's with babies in their arms. The butcher came running out of his shop with a leg of mutton in his hand, and Miss Rose, who didn't appear offended after all, gamely took Eliza in her arms. The news spread from around us and seemed to bring out every able-bodied person in the village. Meanwhile, I was relieved to find that Holmes was now the one with the gun, and as my eyes scanned the mayhem, I saw the hapless Clarke and his assistant skulking away at the back of the crowd.

"Stop the doctor and Mrs Parkfield!" I screamed as loudly as I could, no longer caring how insane I might or might not seem. "They killed Phillimore!" As could be expected, this assertion produced a flurry of aimless noise and activity, but thankfully, a young man with strong arms and an equally strong mind laid hold of the man, and his action prompted the vicar, who was next to him, to take hold of Mrs Parkfield's wrists. Edward Rayburn looked nothing like a knight in shining armor, but as he paraded Dr Clarke over to Holmes, he looked as heroic as any subject of a romantic painting that I had ever seen. Father Murphy seemed less comfortable with the task of dragging a substantial, angry woman in our direction, but he did so.

At that moment, someone in the crowd screamed, "There's a real fire!" and I realised that I had actually managed to forget the flames that Holmes had set on their merry way.

"The fire brigade must form immediately," said Holmes, "and Miss Adler, Edward Rayburn, and the vicar will help me restrain these two until the police arrive." The sound of my friend's commanding voice worked wonders among the crowd, who almost magically broke apart to follow his instructions.

The detective led the group of captives and captors to the village green, where the Winking Tree greeted us with its usual green solemnity. "This will be best," said Holmes. "Impossible to escape in plain sight with the whole village outside." He sounded, I thought, quite pleased. "Now, we will send to the farm for the inspector and sergeant," he continued.

"I could drive Miss Adler," said an eager voice, and I looked behind me to find that Jimmy Simms, a young man possessed of dimples and oversized hands, had run over and was eagerly awaiting instructions like an energetic puppy.

"Very well," said Holmes, "but first, fetch us some rope." The boy was quick, and in a few minutes, the resolute Edward and tired vicar were relieved of the task of subduing Clarke and Mrs Parkfield.

———

"How did Mr Holmes get them?" asked Simms eagerly once we were on our way.

"He surprised them," I answered, "by starting the fire."

The boy's eyes grew large with amazement. "He might have gotten burned himself."

"That's true," I answered. I hadn't thought of it until then.

Chance has put in our way a most singular and whimsical problem, and its solution is its own reward.

—The Adventure of the Blue Carbuncle

Chapter 16: Holmes

Inspector Graves and Sergeant Chipping arrived as quickly as Holmes had expected. Behind them, Simms drove Irene's wagon, but crowded in with The Woman were Edith Phillimore, Julia Rayburn, and an unhappy Mrs. Merriwether.

The first thing out of anyone's mouth was Edith Phillimore's hasty cry of "Where's Eliza?"

"Right here, Love," said Miss Rose, who'd stepped into the open door of the butcher shop with her precious bundle once the fire was out and the crowd dispersed. The child was still drowsy, but she was awake enough to smile at her mother and cling to her neck.

Meanwhile, Inspector Graves and Sergeant Chipping came over to the Winking Tree, where Holmes was still holding Clarke's handgun on the woman and the doctor. "You're sure, are you?" Graves asked, as if he half hoped Holmes might not be.

"The man confessed as much," said The Woman, coming up behind him, short and determined. "He tried to force Holmes to implicate Charles Stevenson."

Holmes's eyes scanned the group that had gathered around and noticed that Julia Rayburn was extremely pale. "Perhaps," he said, "we might discuss this further inside."

"My parents' home will suffice, I think," said Julia.

"Clarke's no longer will, I fear," said Holmes. "The damage was extensive." Irene, who was at his elbow, looked vastly pleased.

The group made its way into the Stevenson home and were set up in the drawing room.

In his pompous way, Inspector Graves began to question the suspects one by one—first Mrs Parkfield, then

Clarke—taking them from the room almost ceremoniously. Meanwhile, the Stevensons' cook managed to produce enough tea for the impromptu guests, though the footmen looked as if they thought those they served were beneath them.

Within a short time, a tall, elegant figure appeared. Charles Stevenson, barrister, arrived home to find his house overrun with all manner of people and glowered at them all.

He came toward the detective, who was seated on a sofa with The Woman and Edith Phillimore, who held her sleepy daughter in her arms. "You'll never convict my friend," he said sharply. "The case will be fought at every turn."

"I highly doubt it will be so difficult," said Holmes mildly. The barrister's rancor, he thought, stemmed from his realisation that he had been a strong suspect. The detective wondered what he knew of his daughter's situation and concluded that he seemed to know nothing at all.

After a long time, Sergeant Chipping emerged with Clarke; behind them was Inspector Graves, whose eyes blazed. He pointed a long finger at the cowering Mrs Merriwether who, during the proceedings, had tried to seem as if she was invisible. "You," he said, "come with us." Mrs Parkfield, restrained under many watchful eyes, looked slightly triumphant as the corpulent woman was led away to be questioned.

Under cover of the excited and speculative conversation that followed, Irene turned to Holmes and spoke softly. "What has she to do with it? She helped the Phillimores with their plan, but Clarke would have no knowledge of that. I thought you took her admission of Phillimore's unfaithfulness as proof of her innocence."

"I suspect," the detective answered, "that she had nothing to do with the murder itself, but anything else would not surprise me. Phillimore was a small man."

The Woman looked irritated at the incompleteness of this speech, but Holmes turned to Edith and reassured her that if the cook was innocent, he would see to it that she was found so. The fact that he thought her far from innocent did not change the truth of the statement.

The final person Sergeant Chipping fetched was the white-faced and shaky-handed Julia Rayburn, though he did not return Mrs Merriwether to the gathering. As the girl walked across the plush carpet, all eyes in the room followed her, most with surprise, but a few with understanding. Holmes had noticed that she had neither spoken to her husband nor taken her seat with him.

Predictably, the barrister exploded at the perceived injustice. "What do they mean taking my Julia? What could she possibly have to do with it?"

"She's the reason for the whole thing," said Mrs. Parkfield, insinuating nastily.

Suddenly, Edward Rayburn rose to his full height and looked her in the eyes. "That's my wife you're talking about."

"Wife," she replied with an ugly laugh, but at the same time, she retreated into herself and held her tongue as if his vehemence frightened her. Characteristic, Holmes thought, of the sort of person so under another's spell that she would do what Mrs. Parkfield had done that day, the kind of person who only felt strong with gun in hand. Clarke sat silent, as he had the entire time he was not being questioned.

After a very long time, Julia finally emerged, and it was obvious she had been weeping. Edward went to her and took her hand. She did not pull away, and she did not speak.

The Inspector, the Sergeant, and Mrs Merriwether came out at last, and Graves went over to Holmes and held out his hand. "I'll shake your hand, Sir," he said. "You know I'm not fond of you from way back, but I acknowledge our indebtedness."

Recognising the immense effort it took for the man to swallow his pride, Holmes stood and took the hand that was proffered, shaking it firmly. Sergeant Chipping beamed like a large, slow sun, and as Holmes sat down, Irene gave him an ungenteel look that he could only interpret as a wink.

———

If the proceedings had begun dramatically, they ended without much fanfare at all. The policemen took Mrs Merriwether, Mrs Parkfield, and Dr Clarke with them, and the rest dispersed slowly, leaving the barrister's house as if bidding goodbye to a ceremony. Irene, Holmes saw, spoke quietly to a few people, though he did not know her purpose. Once outside, she slipped her hand in his arm.

"Holmes," she said, as they made their way back to the cottage, "you are a braver man than even I realised."

"What do you mean?" he asked. "You were calm enough in peril. Never lost your nerve."

"I mean—I mean the fire. You could have been injured or killed very easily."

"That was no matter," said the detective. "I was thinking of the child."

"But how did you do it? I confess my observational skills were eclipsed by my shock and panic."

163

"A white phosphorous match and alcohol are not the best of combinations at any time," said Holmes. "With a bit of a nudge, they are lethal. Nevertheless, I don't think Clarke was terribly sorry to be found out. For all his posturing, I think he's proud of his work."

"But why do it?" asked The Woman. "What did he have against Phillimore? Stevenson's potential motive was far more penetrable."

"Indeed," said Holmes. "My observation tells me that his decision had to do with Julia Rayburn."

"Does the whole world revolve around Julia Rayburn?" Irene exploded. "The poor girl seems to be at the centre of everything."

"Not, perhaps," said Holmes, "the actions of Mrs Merriwether."

"No?" Irene enquired, "after the past few days, I would believe any connection."

"I believe we will find," said Holmes, "that her complicity sprang from an unhealthy devotion to Edith Phillimore."

"Not unlike Mrs Parkfield's to the doctor, then."

"No, I believe Mrs Parkfield is in love with her employer, while at the same time deploring his hold over her. She's an interesting specimen. The psychologists of London would find her an engaging study."

"I am sorry," said Irene, "that your old friend is the guilty party."

"One can hardly call a man one only knew before the age of twelve to be an old friend, however much he wishes it. I see now that his kindness was meant to forestall discovery."

"Abominable," said The Woman, and her tone of voice made Holmes afraid that she might wrap her arms around him as she had done once during the Florida case. Fortunately, propriety reigned, and she simply gave him her most brilliant smile, a gift, he knew, that most men found priceless.

"The truly abominable thing," said Holmes, "is that I trusted him. It was unforgivable."

"You didn't ultimately trust him," said Irene. "Your instincts led you to the answer." But Holmes was unable to take such a sanguine view of his own behaviour.

"His assessment of the body gave no reason to doubt him," said the detective with irritation. "The preposterous nature of Edith Phillimore's tale prejudiced me against the man as a suspect, and my association with him finished the job."

"I don't suppose it helps any," said The Woman, "but Julia's part in the tale had me looking in other quarters. At one time, the thought even crossed my mind that Edward Rayburn might have done it to avenge Julia's honour."

"It was to your credit," said Holmes, "that you did not disqualify a man you obviously admire."

"Nevertheless," she rejoined, "I cannot think ill of you for taking longer to impute the guilt of a heinous crime onto someone whose methods and kindness were significant to your boyhood." Holmes didn't answer because they were at the cottage, and music was issuing forth from it.

The detective and The Woman found Watson sitting in a chair by the piano, clapping enthusiastically to the merry tune Mrs Turner played. She had on a long, violet dress, the likes of which Holmes had never seen her wear in his long years of association with her, and her hair, which was usually pulled back tightly, was softer this evening and framed her face like a halo. Her fingers ceased moving across the piano keys as they entered.

"Good evening," said Watson, smiling with colour in his cheeks. "Have you been able to advance the case?"

"Upon my word," said Holmes, "where have the two of you been?" He looked over at the housekeeper and saw her simultaneously blush and smile.

"We took a long walk on the Downs," said Watson. "The weather was nice, and we lost track of time. We've only been back a half hour."

"Obviously," Irene interjected. "I'm afraid, Mrs Turner, that I shall have to ask for your assistance. I've done something a bit impulsive and invited guests for an evening meal."

Mrs Turner looked surprised for a moment, and then she stood up with resolve. "As you know," she said, "I am more than equal to the task."

"I believe you," said Irene, "but I insist on helping, just this once. I was in peril for my life a short time ago. You might take pity on me." She grinned saucily at the older woman.

"As you wish, Miss Adler," the cook and housekeeper answered as her mouth tried to curve into a smile. Holmes realised then what Irene's whispers to various and sundry had been about.

The two women disappeared into the kitchen, and Holmes took his place in the wing chair opposite his flatmate, who had moved to the sofa. "Well, Holmes," said Watson, "I had no idea things would erupt in this manner. I apologise for my absence."

"No need," said the detective. "Miss Adler was adequate, though she lacks your physical instincts."

"A woman of her appearance needs no physical instincts," Watson answered, "so capable is she of engendering them in others on her behalf."

"Perhaps," said Holmes, "though I deduce that you are unaffected by her."

"My attentions go another way," said the doctor placidly, "but that is hardly important at the moment. My own limping effort at deduction finds from your manner and Miss Adler's that the case is solved."

"It is," said Holmes, "though it reflects little credit on my career."

"I doubt that," said Watson.

"Well," said the detective, "dinner will assuage your curiosity."

"That process," said I, "starts upon the supposition that when you have eliminated all which is impossible, then whatever remains, however improbable, must be the truth."

—The Blanched Soldier

Chapter 17: Irene

The surpassing simplicity of the instructions Mrs Turner gave me as we cooked and set the table had the effect of making me feel like a slow-witted child. "I'm not a fine lady," I finally said to her. "I've done these things for myself before."

"You've never been in service," she retorted.

"Very well," I acquiesced. I might be able to keep my wits about me when a gun was pointed in my direction, but I was hopeless in the face of my housekeeper's endless determination. I couldn't blame her when I saw the spread that she somehow managed to produce, consisting of sausage pies, potatoes, cabbage, and several other bits and bobs that made my mouth water. Sometimes, I was very glad I'd left the life of a professional touring singer behind.

My small party of guests arrived on time for our late meal. Edward Rayburn and the vicar came in together, followed by Simms, and finally Edith, Eliza and Julia. Edith and I quickly took Eliza and put her to bed in the housekeeper's room, where she had previously spent the night. Her ordeal and drugging, which turned out to be via a non-harmful sedative, had made her extremely tired, and she was delighted to fall asleep with Charles the rabbit in her arms.

When Julia saw her husband already present, I thought she might refuse to stay, but as I had hoped, she dreaded a scandal too much to run away. Perhaps it was unforgivably high-handed of me, but I could not resist a last effort to unite the couple. I knew that Julia intended to leave the village as soon as the police told her she might, and I couldn't stand the idea. Edward, I thought, had come to town expressly to plead with her; he'd have had no other reason to leave his farm. Judging by their looks at one another, it seemed that he had not succeeded in seeing her.

So far, I thought, Julia's predicament was known to only a few. How it could continue to be concealed, I couldn't fathom, but I trusted that Holmes would do his best to see that it was. My friend had no aversion to seeing the guilty punished to the full extent of the law, but he was always careful to protect those who had been brought into cases through the crimes of others.

My small table was hardly big enough for the eight of us to sit around while Mrs Turner served us, but we managed it, and the close quarters seemed to contribute to a more convivial atmosphere. There was a certain air of relief that pervaded the company at knowing, come what may, that the man responsible for the death of James Phillimore was in the hands of the police. The man's disappearance had hung like a spectre over the village, and it was as if Holmes's fire had been a cleansing one, ridding Fulworth of its confusion and fear.

I wasn't consciously thinking these things, though, as we sat down to Mrs Turner's sumptuous meal. I was merely thinking of how famished I was, and I didn't seem to be the only one. For the first time in days, Holmes really ate, and I relished the sight. Watson, too, showed his appreciation of Mrs Turner's cooking by partaking of a great deal of it. Simms was the most openly appreciative, remarking constantly about how wonderful everything was. I doubted that, as a shop boy, he was used to being invited out very often, and he seemed determined to savour the occasion as thoroughly as possible. I knew that he enjoyed my company and, perhaps, fancied me a bit, but I didn't mind.

"I would like to propose a toast," I said after a while, "to our friends, who helped us solve the case."

"The credit goes to Mr Holmes, surely," said Edith.

"In this instance, I believe Mr Holmes is happy to share it with all of you." I couldn't help the slight smirk that reached my face when I looked across the table at my friend.

"Certainly," he said. "You have all been exceedingly helpful." He was relaxed, I could see, far more so than he had been since his arrival in the village.

"To all of us, then," said the vicar, and we drank. As I looked around the table at the strange assortment of people I'd collected, the warmth I felt surprised me. For the years I had been in Fulworth, I had kept mostly to myself, only coming to know people as I encountered them in my official capacity as musician or in my daily errands.

The trust Edith Phillimore and Julia Rayburn, even Julia's husband, had placed in me during the case had proven to me that I had not made as little impression on the village as I'd supposed. Holmes was fond of saying that when one gets rid of the impossible, whatever remains must be true, no matter how difficult to believe. It was now impossible for me to believe that I meant nothing to the village of Fulworth, and it had begun to seem as if, no matter how much I might deny it to myself, the truth was that Fulworth was also important to me. Perhaps, I thought, I needed people after all.

———

The late hour meant that the guests were not inclined to linger. The vicar left first, with many expressions of thanks and good will, to return home, where he cared for his ailing mother. Edith soon made to follow, and she went to

171

retrieve her sleeping offspring, who waved to us all from her mother's shoulder and smiled as if she'd never had a care in the world. Simms would have stayed to eat and drink all night, I believe, except that the family for whom he worked kept strict hours, and he did not wish to upset them. He kissed my hand as he left, slightly overcome by the atmosphere and his overconsumption of my highest quality wine, opened especially for the occasion.

Finally, Julia and Edward were the only ones left, and it was obvious that neither wanted to be the first to leave, for which I was glad. "Julia," I said as we sat together on the sofa, "I am curious if you know more about the case than I do. I understand who is responsible, but I don't know how it was done."

Julia looked around at the small, informal gathering sitting on sofa and chairs pulled from the table to accommodate our extra visitors. It was just me, Holmes, Watson, and Edward to listen to her now, and I saw a decision cross her face.

"I expect everyone here already knows my— situation, since you have all been assisting the police. I believe it will be good for me to tell what I know, and it's the least I can do. The police were able to piece together most of what happened from the stories of the two women and the doctor." I patted her hand as if I was her aged grandmother. I couldn't help myself. Meanwhile, Edward watched her with one of the most intense gazes I have ever seen coming from anyone other than Sherlock Holmes.

"As you know, Miss Adler," she said, looking at me as if for support, "I have an unusual relationship with the servants at my childhood home. I think, perhaps, you did not think my behaviour was entirely wise, and experience bears you out. One of them, I don't know which, saw me speaking with James Phillimore outside the servants' entrance to the house. The encounter so inflamed her with curiosity that she followed us and found out that we—the character of our relationship." I shuddered internally at the implication, and Edward Rayburn looked as if he was in pain so acute he could no longer keep it from showing on his honest face.

"This person," Julia continued, "had a friendship with Mrs Merriwether at Oakhill Farm, and she took the tale to that lady, who was furious on account of her love for Edith Phillimore, whom she saw as a wronged woman. She's the one who told Dr Clarke." I had been listening intently, but this piece of information piqued my interest in the extreme. Now, I thought, we would find out if Holmes was correct in his surmise that Phillimore's murder had had something to do with Julia Rayburn.

Julia took a sip of her drink and waited a moment to continue. "I don't suppose it should bother me to tell the rest," she said, "since I've no reputation left anyway, but it still pains me to say. When I first returned from school, I noticed that Dr Clarke paid special attention to me. I thought it was just the affection of an old man, since he had always been fond of me when I was a child. However, before James had even spoken to me, the doctor approached me after church. He was a widower, he said, but he wanted— someone to share his life again, perhaps to give him the family in his old age that the wife of his youth had not been able to produce. You may imagine the effect of his words. I felt dreadful and filled with pity that I couldn't entirely conceal. As gently as I could, I told him that I did not consider myself equal to what he asked. I was barely past being a child, I said, and couldn't think of fulfilling his request. A month later, he asked again. That time, I told him more strongly that while I respected him, I did not care for him in that way. He never spoke to me again."

"I never told my father or anyone else because I wanted to spare the man's feelings, but his attentions had not gone entirely unnoticed. I did not know it then, but Mrs Parkfield was aware of his regard for me, and she was angry because she had long dreamed of becoming the second Mrs Clarke. She, too, was friends with Mrs Merriwether, who seems to have been apprised of any and all gossip among servants in the area. Mrs Parkfield told her friend what Dr Clarke's intentions were toward me."

"Mrs Merriwether held onto the information, as she must have held on to all sorts of scandal and gossip that might be embarrassing or damaging to a great many people. When she heard about James and me, she decided to make use of the knowledge. She went to Dr Clarke under guise of subservient friendship and told him that the object of his affection was being tampered with." Julia said this last part as if it was difficult for her to form the words.

"She had judged her man accurately. I had thought Dr Clarke had accepted my choice as a gentleman, but he was secretly obsessed. I have heard it said that he was possessive and unusually jealous where his first wife was concerned, but I was too young then to know for sure. In the months since I'd refused him, he'd grown increasingly unbalanced, and Mrs Merriwether only had to push him slightly to get him to act. She didn't intend to push him into murder, or so she claims. She only wanted Phillimore to leave so that she could convince Edith to rid herself of him. She suggested blackmail."

I looked at Holmes, who was as intent on the story as I was. "The blackmail was real, then."

174

"Yes," said my friend. "It was simply the subject that Phillimore fabricated."

"Clarke told him he must leave the village, or all would be known," said Julia.

"Not about money, then," Holmes murmured. "I thought that was the least plausible part of Edith's story."

"According to Mrs Merriwether," Julia continued, "Phillimore sent a letter to Clarke agreeing to leave, and then, of course, he convinced his wife to help him, with the object of rejoining him later. The cook thought she could dissuade Edith from this once she disclosed the truth. Clarke, however was not satisfied with the man merely leaving Fulworth."

"He had—seen what my husband saw. After all, he has been a doctor for many years, and he watched me. He began to suspect the truth about the baby, and it filled him with jealousy. On the pretext of making Phillimore prove that he was actually leaving, he asked for the particulars of the man's plan. Phillimore, who was terrified that his actions would become known and that he would lose his wife and daughter, complied."

"On the day of my wedding," she said, pausing a moment and breathing heavily, "husband and wife followed the plan to the letter. James went inside to fetch his umbrella and never came back. Edith followed, but she did not look through the house, since she knew her husband was simply lying in wait. They had arranged for the property to be deserted after Edith's departure, so James lingered and then made his escape."

"Dr Clarke was aware of the details of the plan, so he had already circulated the information that he was laid up with gout and would be unable to attend the wedding. He and Mrs Parkfield waited for James on the road outside the

175

village, and they drugged him and brought him back to Clarke's house, where they kept him sedated for several days. The doctor, of course, has access to all manner of drugs."

"Mrs Merriwether faked the posting of the rabbit both ways. She apparently tried to extricate herself when Clarke told her that he had kidnapped Phillimore instead of letting him leave as they'd agreed, but he threatened to bring her down with him if she did not do as he asked."

"Finally, when the police had begun to talk about ending the investigation because of insignificant evidence, Clarke shot James. I do not—I do not know exactly how or where he did it. The police believe he took him out on the Downs."

"Horrible," I said.

"Yes," said Julia. "I would not have wished such an end on him."

"Clarke was then," she added, "faced with the task of what to do with the body. He was highly unbalanced by this time, and he wanted to display what he had done as revenge against the man he believed had stolen the woman he loved. He could not contrive a way to do it himself, so he called on Mrs Merriwether again. This time, she claims, she very nearly refused, but she was terrified that Clarke would convince the police that she had killed Phillimore, since the plot had originated with her. Of course, Clarke would probably have gotten away with it if he'd just discarded the corpse somewhere on the Downs, but he could not be satisfied with that."

"The night before the body was found, Mrs Merriwether went to Clarke's house in her husband's wagon. Mrs Parkfield helped her load Phillimore's corpse into it, covered by a blanket and then various edibles, so that if pressed, she could claim she was taking supplies back for the big house."

"She had told her husband that Edith Phillimore wished her to remain at the house later than usual, so under cover of night, she placed the body on the carriage and then went home and to bed. Clarke had told her that the police would never suspect that a woman had done it, which was true. Only one as strong as she is could have managed it, aided by the fact that James was a slight man."

"Mrs Merriwether received quite a turn the next morning when Edith Phillimore told her the body had been found by Eliza. She'd hoped that the location of the carriage house would lead to its being found by one of the men and that Warren would be suspected. She convinced Edith, who was shocked and fearful because of her own duplicity, that it would be better to wait and let him be found by someone else, which soon happened."

"There you have it," said Julia, sitting back wearily. I almost laughed. It was such an oddly anticlimactic end to a tale of horror. We sat silently for a few moments, thinking about the ending of a man's life and the sad circumstances that had led him to it, not that none of them were of his own making—far from it.

After a while, Dr Watson rose, rubbing his eyes. "Thank you for enlightening us so fully," he said to Julia. "Forgive me, Miss Adler," he continued, "but I must retire, or I will be snoring into my cups." I nodded and stood up, and Holmes and the Rayburns followed suit. "I'd better go, too," said Julia.

"Jule," said Edward, and he put out a tentative hand to touch her hair. She flinched. I gave Holmes and Watson meaningful looks, and they disappeared into their rooms. I, too, retired, but instead of disappearing altogether, I sneaked into the shadows of the hallway and ducked behind the chaise longue with my head just peeking up enough to see what took place. I am not proud of this, but I'm not terribly sorry, either. I simply could not resist.

"Where are you going?" Edward asked, once they were alone.

"I'll stay one more night with my father and mother and then leave for London tomorrow."

"Do I get no say?" he asked desperately. "I feel—the same for you that I've always felt."

"How is that possible, Ed?" she asked. "Do you understand what this means? I courted you on purpose just so I could marry you quickly and cover my shame. I used your love for me as a means to an end." She spoke vehemently, as if she was determined to condemn herself as fully as possible.

"I know all that, Jule," he answered, "but I think you love me. Look at me and say you don't."

She made a valiant effort, and I was afraid that if she succeeded, she might very well have gotten her way that night. As it was, she couldn't meet his eyes and tell the lie. "I can't," she said in a short, brittle voice.

"I thought not," he said, sounding more hopeful.

"What is the matter with you?" Julia asked. "I'm carrying a dead man's baby."

"It could be our baby," he said.

"Are you insane?" she asked. "You know what they'll say about us, about you."

"I don't care," he answered calmly.

"Why?" she asked, finally exploding. "I'm not worth this, Ed. I've never been worth all of your love and faithfulness and kindness." She spit out the words as if they were pejorative rather than complimentary. "I've never done anything but stomp on them."

"But you love me, Jule," he said. "Can't you see it in yourself? You love me so much it's nearly killing you to let me go." His eyes shone with tears.

Julia let out a pained cry and buried her face in her hands, though she did not weep. She simply stood silent and refused to look at her husband. "Why?" she finally said. "Why must you be so right and know everything?"

"I know you," he said. "That's all."

"I want you to love someone else," she said stubbornly.

"I've never loved anybody else," he said. Julia turned away.

Edward cried. I have seen men cry for effect, and I have seen them cry like lost children. He did neither. He cried like someone who hurts so deeply for another that the pain cannot be contained.

"Ed—stop," said Julia, finally sounding desperate instead of resigned. "I can't bear it."

"Do you think I can bear it?" he asked, talking to her back. "Do you think I can stand to watch you sacrifice yourself, alone without anyone to help you? We can live like brother and sister if you wish it. I will give up every other dream I've ever had if you'll just let me take care of you and the baby."

For a long, horrendous moment, I was afraid that Julia was going to run away. Her internal conflict was excruciatingly visible, but Edward was wise enough to let her make the decision on her own terms. She finally crumbled, collapsing into herself and sobbing so hard she bent double. The farmer recognised her choice for what it was, and he came to her in an instant, catching her and

179

pulling her close. "I've got you," was all he said, but in spite of his tears, he looked happier than I had ever seen him. He held her for a long time, only stopping when her sobs subsided, and even then, he only let go so that he could take out a red handkerchief and wipe away her final tears. His wife, in her turn, took the piece of cloth from him and wiped his face.

"Julia," he said, cupping her face in one of his broad hands, "will you really come home with me?"

"If you want me to," she said.

"I want—I want you to come home more than I ever wanted anything in my whole life," he answered, and I was afraid they were both in danger of weeping again. Instead, Edward put a big arm around Julia's shoulders and led her out into the night.

I watched the Rayburns leave my cottage with no idea what lay in store for their future. I have not always been a hopeful person, but I hoped for them. Julia did not deserve Edward after everything she had done to him, but, as I pondered then, life would be a terrible thing if we all received our just deserts. Holmes would disagree on principle, I thought, but that would make him the greatest of hypocrites. He was, after all, the man who had given a cottage to his enemy and made her his friend.

They can go everywhere, see everything, overhear everyone.

—The Sign of Four

Chapter 18: Holmes

The detective slept all night, finally giving his body the rest it craved. When he awoke, he realised it was late morning, and he heard the voices of The Woman and the doctor in the main part of the house.

"Good morning, Holmes," said Irene when he emerged. She looked fresh and rested, though he knew that the case had taken a toll on her as well, a toll that was now evaporating in the aftermath of success. The detective sat down beside her at the table and proceeded to avail himself of the large brunch Mrs Turner had provided. Far from being averse to a good meal, he simply found food a largely irrelevant distraction when a case was on. Now, he was free to fill his stomach.

His mind, however, was not entirely engaged in pleasant matters, and he sank into silence as he pondered his failure to put together the details that had implicated Dr Clarke as quickly as he believed he should have done. He had seen the tobacco and the man; that should have been enough, without the kidnapping to serve as a catalyst.

"You are very quiet, Holmes," said Watson after a while. The detective was surprised his flatmate had noticed, so taken up as he seemed with watching Mrs Turner bring food and drinks back and forth from the kitchen. "I'd have expected," the doctor continued, "to hear about Brahms or Greek sculpture or some other obscure topic."

"Brahms is hardly obscure," said Irene, and the detective cast an approving eye on her.

"I committed an error of judgement," said Holmes. "That is all."

As if she knew that nothing could really ease the blow but couldn't help saying something, The Woman said,

"You did something perfectly natural. You trusted someone you had trusted in your youth."

"Natural, perhaps," he rejoined, "but not forgivable."

"Still," she answered, "I don't see that there's any harm done. The murderer is behind bars, and Eliza Phillimore is safe. The loss of the man's house seems more like poetic justice than anything else. As they say, all's well that ends well."

"Convenient platitudes or not, my blundering has wasted time and put a great many people in danger," Holmes lamented.

"I am determined to see the bright side," she retorted. "The case is solved, and your bravery has restored a child to her mother." She smiled wickedly. "You are a hero whether you wish to be or no."

"Frailty, thy name is Sherlock," said the detective, sardonically misusing the words of the Bard.

"I agree with Miss Adler," said Watson gallantly. "You can hardly call a case a failure when it yields a conclusion as excellent as this one." Looking at the glow on the doctor's face, it was obvious that the perceived positive outcomes of his visit were not only related to the case. Holmes grew silent then, but he did not entirely deplore the praise of his friends, however much he might wish to appear that he did.

"Clarke is a fool," Irene said.

"Not a fool," Holmes rejoined. "He miscalculated. Without me, he'd probably have gotten away with it."

"I'm sure Inspector Graves is delighted to have to confront that reality," The Woman answered.

"I can't help feeling a small amount of pity for the doctor," said Watson. "He really seems to have loved the girl, however misguidedly."

"I don't," Irene answered, more sharply than he deserved. "Clarke's love is the sort that holds so tightly it chokes, rather than letting the object of its affection grow and thrive." As the detective watched her, he understood. When she saw Clarke in her mind, Holmes thought, instead of his own, he wore the face of Godfrey Norton, her late husband.

"What I don't understand," Watson added, "is why Stevenson went to the Merriwether home at all. You considered it highly suspicious at the time."

Holmes smiled sardonically. "The answer is quite prosaic. The barrister's wife suffers from chronic headaches, and Mrs Merriwether is known to dispense herbal remedies, which Mrs Stevenson does not trust the servants to procure for her."

"It's satisfying to know the answer, at least," said The Woman. Watson nodded complacently.

"Will you add this story to your collection of tales, Dr Watson?" Irene finally asked.

"I think not," he replied, "though the sensational nature of the case is appealing, purely from an objective standpoint. Nevertheless, I would not like to offend Edith or Eliza by providing a written reminder of their tragedy. If I ever do write it, I will change the particulars of the case, something I have been known to do before that never fails to irritate my friend." Holmes shook his head.

"I will," continued Dr Watson, "treat the case as a disappearance that was never solved. I can't think that it is bad for my friend's vanity to be thought fallible on occasion."

"In this case," said Holmes glumly, "you could hardly paint me as more fallible than I have been."

"Nonsense," said Watson.

Holmes lingered at the table for a long time, letting himself enjoy the company of The Woman, his flatmate, and the housekeeper. He thought he might stay one more day in Fulworth, enjoying the air and companionship, before returning to the equally desired smells and sights of London, where the police could contact him if they desired his evidence. He had begun to think that he might retire some day. When he'd bought the cottage, the idea had been so far off as to be almost unreal. So, too, when he had given the property to Irene Adler after the case that had made them friends. Now he could begin to see an end to his career, though it did not yet beckon him. He was still intoxicated by his metropolitan mistress, and he could not bear to cease savouring her delights just yet.

The detective's pondering was cut short by a ring of Irene's bell. Mrs Turner opened the door to reveal Eliza and Edith Phillimore, who held out a cake wrapped in brown paper. "I don't know how to thank you," said the mother, "but this is Lewis's special recipe. She's turned out to be quite a cook, now that Mrs Merriwether is gone."

"Thank you," said Irene, taking the parcel and smiling at the sweet smell that issued forth from it. "I'll make sure Mr Holmes has a bit."

"Eliza has a different gift for him," said Edith, pushing her daughter forward gently. Holmes rose and stood in front of her,

With an intensely serious expression, Eliza held out her rabbit, her one prized possession in the whole world, toward Holmes. "You take him," she said.

The detective stared down at her for a long moment, unable to assimilate the immensity of her offering. Finally, he knelt down in front of her and took the toy from her hand. He held it to his ear. "I'm afraid I mustn't take

Charles," he said. "He doesn't want to move to Baker Street. He'd rather stay with you."

Eliza stared hard, then took the rabbit back and held it to her own ear. "He says his name isn't Charles any more," she said firmly. "He says his name is Mr Holmes." With that, she wrapped her arms around the neck of the still-kneeling detective and kissed his thin cheek. His smile revealed that he did not mind.

"Eliza," he said after a moment, "would you like to be a Baker Street Irregular?"

"What is that?" she asked, staring at him intently.

"A group of very clever children who help me solve crimes," he answered.

"But I don't live on Baker Street," she said, perplexed.

"No," said Holmes, "but you can be an Irregular wherever you live."

"How?" she asked, clearly excited.

"By keeping your eyes and ears open and learning as much as you can about the world around you," said Holmes.

"Oh," she said, as if this wasn't quite as enthralling as she'd anticipated.

Holmes touched the tip of her nose with his long index finger. "You have much to learn, and if I ever see you again, I expect to find out that you've made good use of your time." He leaned toward her conspiratorially. "After all, Miss Eliza, you never know when the smallest detail will solve the biggest case." This statement produced a delighted grin on Eliza's face. The detective took her hand and kissed it before standing to his feet once again.

Few people ever credited Holmes with such sentimentality. Then again, if they had read Dr Watson's description of the ragtag group of children he employed, children who followed him year upon year, they should have known.

The Woman installed the mother and child on the sofa, and Mrs Turner brought tea for Edith and milk for Eliza, who lapped it up as eagerly as a kitten and seemed very well pleased. "I cannot fail to tell you, Edith, how grateful I am at your reception of Julia Rayburn," said Irene quietly. "You would have been justified in a much different response."

"Perhaps it was stupid of me," said Edith, staring down at her hands, "but I forgave her immediately. She's so pale and so young and afraid. I think she's terrified of what will happen if her father finds out. So far, the police have agreed to conceal as much of the matter as they can, and I hope, for both our sakes, that they will be able to do so."

"You are a far from ordinary person, Mrs Phillimore," said Holmes.

"Thank you, Mr Holmes," she answered. "I am proud of my actions, even though they must never be known. I am not, however, proud of the deceit that began the nightmare," she said, "and I thank you for keeping it hidden."

"No reason to reveal it now," said Holmes, "since it has nothing whatsoever to do with the outcome of the case, and Clarke had no idea James had brought you in on the matter. I am only sorry it took me so long to solve the case that Eliza was put in peril."

"It's all right," said Eliza, suddenly looking up from her cup. "I had Mr Holmes to protect me," and she hugged the bedraggled white rabbit delightedly. A stuffed rabbit might have limitations of ability, Holmes thought, but it was hardly deficient in loyalty and faithfulness. In the main, he was pleased by the comparison.

Edith continued a moment later, "We'll be leaving Fulworth soon. I don't believe it's fair to either of us to remain. I have a sister in London, and we'll sell the farm and join her. That will also help to keep—Julia's matter from becoming as widely known, I think, but don't imagine that I'm being ridiculously self-sacrificing." She smiled at the detective. "Mr Holmes, you've had no occasion to see me as I usually am, but I dearly love a party, and Louisa promises me she'll quickly get our minds off our troubles."

The Woman hugged both mother and daughter before they left, and Holmes saw tears in her eyes when she straightened back up. They suited her, he thought, and gave her a softness she did not always possess.

He continued to watch her as she stood in the doorway and waved to the retreating figures, and he realised that he had been mistaken. The softness was always there now. He had observed her since his arrival, but he hadn't really looked at her, not enough to consider the implications of how she now appeared. His first visit to Sussex had shown a change in her, a freedom and peacefulness that had been alien to her previously. That transformation had continued. She would never be identical to other women in the village of Fulworth. She was far too American and too much herself for that, but she had a place there now, and within it she was content. Holmes enjoyed watching her.

"It's pleasantly chilly today," she said, finally turning back and closing the door. "Would you like to greet the bees?"

"Certainly," he answered, retrieving his coat. He followed The Woman to the hives and watched her interacting with the bees. She was filled with calm and intuition, perfectly at home among them. That made sense, he thought, for she was one of them. No, not a drone. She was the queen. He had seen through the days of his visit how often the people of Fulworth came to her, consulted her, even loved her. The small cottage on the hill was fast becoming the centre of all things. The charming thing about Irene Adler was that she had no idea. She was a queen who was totally oblivious to the fact that the kingdom was hers.

———

Holmes spent the afternoon reading the London newspapers, which Mycroft had contrived to have delivered to Irene's doorstep. He was glad at such times that he and his brother were at peace with one another. He was frightened by few things, but he did not like to contemplate being in the disfavour of someone so powerful. The detective, of course, had no such desire for power himself. He was quite pleased with his lot.

Finally, when it was nearing time for the evening meal, Watson rose from his place on the sofa, where he had been reading the description of a new discovery called X-radiation, which some were predicting might have vast medical implications in the future. "Holmes," he said, "I've a mind to go down to the inn in the village. Mrs Turner says the apple pie is outstanding. I thought you might wish to accompany me."

"Very well," said Holmes, extracting his long limbs from the wing chair. "I wouldn't object to a drink in your company if Miss Adler doesn't mind us deserting her for the evening."

"Certainly not," said Irene saucily. "I welcome the solitude; it's been hard to come by these past days."

As he closed the cottage door, Holmes heard the sound of a body sliding onto a wooden surface, and the sound of piano music followed. He almost wished he had not agreed to leave.

And when he speaks of Irene Adler, or when he refers to her photograph, it is always under the honourable title of *the* woman.

—A Scandal in Bohemia

Chapter 19: Irene

The two men came back very late in the evening from their visit to the Mountebank Inn and Pub. Watson went to bed immediately, but Holmes joined me, relaxing into the black chair and taking out his pipe. I could finally see the toll exhaustion and hunger had taken on him, and I knew that one day had not been enough time to assuage his body's demands. I wished he would give himself more time to recover from the strain of the case, but I very much doubted that he would do so.

"You must be pleased," he said, closing his eyes and enjoying his tobacco. "You played through your entire repertoire of Bach this evening. Your pleasure, I expect, is due to your success in reuniting the Rayburns." I smiled. Holmes's deductions had become comfortable to me, like an afghan or a pair of old Wellington boots. I liked knowing how they were done, but I could trust him even when he didn't explain his conclusions.

"It was as successful as it could have been, I suppose," I said. "They have a great deal between them."

"Any two people have a great deal between them," Holmes observed. "Some of the most lurid crimes I've ever encountered were between people who appeared to be in simple, straightforward relationships."

"Nothing is straightforward about relationships," I added, smiling. And yet, as I sat opposite Sherlock Holmes, I felt as if we two were the exceptions that proved the rule. We had weathered being enemies, lying to one another, and fighting for our lives. Somehow, we had come out of it all as friends. To the outside eye, it might seem complicated, but it wasn't. He was the detective, and I was The Woman, and it was all, and it was enough.

———

The following morning, Mrs Turner cooked a hearty breakfast to prepare our friends for the journey back to London. As we waited for the table to be set, I sat down beside Dr Watson and could not resist teasing him a bit.

"I take it you and I are likely to be enemies soon," I said.

"Whatever do you mean?" he asked, his kind face turning suddenly pink.

"I refer to the fact that you seem to be on your way to parting me from the best housekeeper and cook on this side of the country."

He smiled beatifically. "I won't deny my intentions. When my Mary died, I never thought I would meet a woman as capable and sensible as she was, and the London girls have proven me sadly right. Unstable, I'm afraid. Mrs Turner is—she's strong and able and quiet, just the sort of woman I'd like to sit with in the evenings by the fireside and talk over the events of the day. A comfortable woman, you understand."

I did understand. Though Mrs Turner was not to every man's taste, she was all the things he said, along with possessing a gentleness of spirit that she took pains to conceal but could not keep from expressing. I approved of the man's choice. Of course, sedateness had never been a quality that particularly attracted me, but I could allow for human differences. It pleased me to think that the easier life the doctor would provide for her would allow for more and more days of violet dresses and handsomely arranged hair and none of having to wait on a flighty singer with eccentric acquaintances. She might, I thought, find the leisure slightly trying, but she would have to work that out with Watson.

―――

"Lewis told me how the Winking Tree got its name," I said as I walked Holmes to the train station later in the day. Mrs Turner and Watson were far behind, deep in congenial conversation with one another, as they attempted to prolong their time together.

"Yes?" said my friend after a while. "I take it you intend to share this information."

I smiled. "You needn't be cross. It's a local story about a beautiful farmer's daughter who fell in love with the son of the richest man in the village. His father forbade him to see her, but the two left each other letters in a hollow of the tree. Others in the village would help the lovers by passing on the message that the tree was winking whenever it contained a note. Finally, after the girl almost died of a fever, the young man's father relented and let him marry her."

"I must say," rejoined my friend drily, "I was expecting something more ancient and tragic than that."

"As soon the young man was married, the young girls of the village began to view the tree as a symbol of passion and to whisper that if a person in love touched its bark, her romance was sure to have a happy ending."

"Villages are hotbeds of such nonsense," said Holmes.

―――

It was twilight when I returned from the train station, and everything in the village was closed, with most of the homes shuttered and quiet for the evening. As I passed the green, I stopped and looked at the Winking Tree, the place where Eliza had spent happy hours with her father and lost her rabbit, the clue that had sent Holmes along the pathway toward the conclusion of the case. The outline of the branches was magnificent against the night sky, and I could almost imagine how the villagers had begun to regard it as lucky or even magical.

The slight breeze through the leaves whispered my name *Irene Adler* on the wind, and I thought of who I was: The Woman, who had known few good men and loved even fewer. I slipped off my shoes and stepped onto the grass, enjoying the sensation on the bottoms of my feet.

I am not normally a fanciful person, but as I walked toward the Winking Tree, its branches seemed like open arms welcoming me into its green and vibrant embrace. I reached forward and touched the tips of my fingers to its rough trunk, and my mind was filled with the face of my friend, the best man I had ever known.

Epilogue: Holmes

The detective read the London papers on his way back to Baker Street, but he silently perceived, as he had before, the look of joyful preoccupation in his flatmate's face that denoted the presence of a strong attachment. It had been that way with others, but never as strongly as with Mary Morstan, as if a part of John Watson's heart had been permanently buried along with his wife's silent form.

This time was different. Holmes considered himself neither a psychologist nor a romantic, but he was a student of human behaviour. He steeled himself for the eventualities of a half-empty flat and evenings spent smoking alone by the fire.

He understood not one whit why a man would voluntarily surrender his freedom to the fragile but iron-willed fingers of a woman. Even Mary, who had been, by most comparisons, an understanding wife, had required Watson at times when Holmes had needed his presence. No woman wanted to be married to a detective, not really.

Women in general, he thought, were different from *The* Woman. She was no less infuriating than any of them, but she was clever. She played The Game, and there was something to be said for that.

Epilogue: Irene

Edith Phillimore sold Oakhill Farm to Peter Warren, who cried when he signed the papers that made it legally his. The widow took her daughter to London, where they were able to settle comfortably on the money she'd made. I received a few letters from her, but they stopped after several months. I heard nothing more of Eliza for many years, until the day that the papers reported her name as part of a group of women who were the first to cast feminine votes in a national election. Holmes, who was beside me when I read the story, declared that it surprised him not at all.

Edward and Julia Rayburn remained at their farm outside Fulworth. In the eyes of all in the village, Julia's baby, a son named Steven, belonged fully to Edward, and her father's reputation did much to counter the few stories that claimed otherwise. Tongues wagged about the exact date of the birth, as they always do in a village, and Edward bore the brunt of all suspicion, as if any shame belonged only to him. Still, I had never seen a man so happy with his lot in life. In time, with the help of a son whose laugh was like music, his wife began to smile again.

About the Author

Amy Thomas met Sherlock Holmes around the age of ten, when she was scared out of her wits by an audio recording of "The Speckled Band." From there, she went on to experience heartbreak on Dr. Watson's behalf, only to be told by her older sister that Sherlock Holmes hadn't died after all. Several years later, the gift of a contemporary novel starring Sherlock Holmes rekindled her love of the detective. She re-read the original stories, and a lifelong passion was born.

Amy is a graduate of Regent University, where she majored in professional communication. When she's not podcasting with the Baker Street Babes or writing a novel, she works as an administrative support professional.

An avid knitter and crocheter, Amy has knitted a deerstalker hat and crocheted miniature versions of Sherlock Holmes, John Watson, and James Moriarty. She also enjoys reading and reviewing Holmes-related literature.

The Baker Street Babes

The Baker Street Babes is an international, all-female podcast started by Sherlockian extraordinaire Kristina Manente. They cover topics as diverse as the illustrations of Sydney Paget and the preservation of Undershaw, Sir Arthur Conan Doyle's home, as well as commenting on all kinds of Holmes-related media.

The Babes' blend of irreverent, witty, and intellectual commentary has won them a devoted and ever-widening group of listeners. They were particularly delighted to be featured on NBC during the 2012 Olympic Games.

www.bakerstreetbabes.com

Also from MX Publishing

MX Publishing is proud to support the campaign to save and restore Sir Arthur Conan Doyle's former home. Undershaw is where he brought Sherlock Holmes back to life, and should be preserved for future generations of Holmes fans.

Save Undershaw   www.saveundershaw.com

Facebook   www.facebook.com/saveundershaw

You can read more about Sir Arthur Conan Doyle and Undershaw in Alistair Duncan's book (share of royalties to the Undershaw Preservation Trust) – An Entirely New Country and in the amazing compilation Sherlock's Home – The Empty House (all royalties to the Trust).

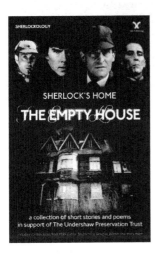

Also from MX Publishing

Sherlock Holmes Travel Guides

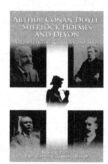

In ebook an interactive guide to London

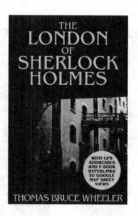

400 locations linked to Google Street View.

Also from MX Publishing

Cross over fiction featuring great villains from history

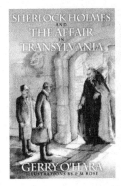
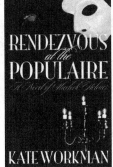

Fantasy Sherlock Holmes

www.mxpublishing.com

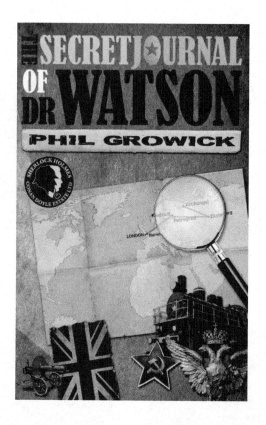

Carrying the seal of the Conan Doyle Estate.....

On the most secret and dangerous assignment of their lives, Sherlock Holmes and Dr. Watson are sent into the newborn Soviet Union to rescue The Romanovs: Nicholas and Alexandra and their innocent children. Will Holmes and Watson be able to change history? Will they even be able to survive?

Also from MX Publishing

The bestselling series featuring a young Winston Churchill

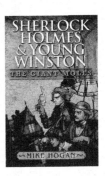

Sherlock Holmes and Young Winston

The Deadwood Stage
The Jubilee Plot
The Giant Moles

"I can tell you straight away the very best thing about this book: there are two more to come in this series. An inspired notion to introduce a young Winston Churchill into the lives of Holmes and Watson and fortunately the inspired writing lives up to that inspired notion. Everything about this book, whether it be plot, casting, characters or dialogue is spot on. Mr Hogan, quite simply, does not put a foot wrong with this volume, roll on the next two."
The Baker Street Society

Also from MX Publishing

When two prison guards are found beheaded in the barren countryside surrounding Her Majesty's Prison at Wormwood Scrubs, Inspector Lestrade seeks Holmes' singular powers to determine how the murders could have been committed in separate locations with the only footprints being those of the murdered guards themselves. With Doctor Watson at his side, Holmes sets out on this new adventure and uncovers deeper mysteries still; mysteries that will not only test the detectives' powers of observation and deduction, but his skepticism of the paranormal as well.

Also from MX Publishing

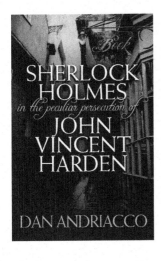 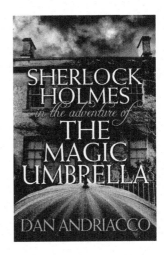

Sherlock Holmes short stories from Dan Andriacco widely
regarded as two of the best pastiches ever written.

Available in all ebook formats including Amazon Kindle,
Kobo and iBooks.

CPSIA information can be obtained
at www.ICGtesting.com
Printed in the USA
FSOW04n2042210116
16081FS